I Should Have Known Better

I Should Have Known Better

William E. Jones

We Heard You Like Books • Los Angeles, California

PUBLISHED BY WE HEARD YOU LIKE BOOKS
A Division of U2603 LLC
5419 Hollywood Blvd, Ste C-231 Los Angeles CA 90027

http://weheardyoulikebooks.com/

Distributed by SCB Distributors

ISBN: 978-0-578-76180-0

Cover photograph: Still from
The Fall of Communism as Seen in Gay Pornography
by William E. Jones, courtesy of the artist
and David Kordansky Gallery.

September 2021

First Edition

10 9 8 7 6 5 4 3 2 1

Hell hath no fury like a failed artist
Or a successful communist.

—"Is It Raining In Your Mouth?"
written by Lias Kaci Saoudi and Saul Adamczewski
recorded by Fat White Family

ONE

"Where are the corporal punishment videos?" asked a man who came into the store just before closing. He spoke in a tentative, high-pitched whine. His heavy-lidded eyes gave him the languid air of someone gradually waking from a deep slumber. Some people would have called his face soulful, like a faithful dog trying to avoid a whipping. I could see that his physique was impressive even though he was fully clothed. He wore a thrift store shirt and shorts with athletic shoes, nothing expensive, so it was difficult to determine his age or social class. He had salt-and-pepper hair, possibly prematurely gray. He wasn't especially tall, but his body took up space in a way that seemed to embarrass him. I couldn't say I was attracted to the man, but I was interested enough that I got up from my seat behind the counter to help him.

I had hoped to see no more customers that evening, and I felt a bit irritated because I was watching a film. The owner of the store wanted videos to be playing on the monitors mounted in a row above the highest shelves; they were meant to show what was available for rent, and they eased the boredom of slow nights. The manager, who had a sentimental side (at least when it came to old movies), had started *Children of Paradise* just before he left for the evening. I became engrossed, and after the first half, I changed the tape—at three hours long, the film had been released as a double vhs. By a quarter to eleven, the end was coming soon, and I didn't want to miss it.

At the back of the maze-like interior of Videoactive, I pointed out the corporal punishment section to the customer, who asked about the relative merits of two titles. I admitted that I wasn't familiar with them. He chose a copy of *Roughed Up Daddies*, and together we walked back to the front counter. I scanned his membership card, and a woman's name appeared on the computer screen in front of me. The address was in Los Feliz, zip code 90027. A second later, a message followed: "Permission to rent for Bernard Kostrovisky." I asked for identification, and he handed me a driver's license bearing the same address.

This customer using a woman's account to rent a gay porn video reminded me of a story told by a friend who used to work as a dominatrix. She often saw a certain type of man who would sit quietly and patiently in the house, waiting for the next client to arrive. He would never say explicitly what he wanted, but as the scene played out, it became clear that he thirsted for another man's cock. The man who waited invariably led a thoroughly conventional life in the suburbs with wife and children, but during the brief period between the end of the work day and the time he caught his train home, he would indulge in his secret desire to perform fellatio. He preferred not to risk being seen at a gay bar or sex club, and fearing arrest, he couldn't bring himself to frequent public lavatories. Because his self-image didn't allow him to pursue his needs by straightforward means, he required my friend to force him to suck cock. That way, as he saw it, he wouldn't be responsible for his actions, because a powerful woman had made him do these things. My dominatrix friend had dealt with many men who fit this description.

With these thoughts in mind, I raised an eyebrow as I looked at Mr. Kostrovisky, and in response, he said, "I'm subletting from a friend."

I nodded. "That'll be $3.50." I thought I saw a similarity between his name and the real surname of a French poet, so I added, "Any relation to Apollinaire?"

He shrugged. "It's the Ellis Island spelling. His ancestors probably owned my ancestors as serfs."

As I gave him change for a $5.00 bill, I noticed that his hands were very large, a little rough, and slightly out of proportion to the rest of his body. At that moment, one of my favorite parts of *Children of Paradise* appeared on the monitor. I instinctively grabbed Kostrovisky's peasant hands and said, "You've got to see this." I turned up the sound, and we watched the scene.

Garance, a former prostitute who lives under the protection of a rich nobleman besotted by her beauty, returns to her opulent Paris residence after an evening at Théâtre des Funambules, where she and her friends had performed years before. She climbs the staircase to her bedroom and stops when a figure from her past, Lacenaire, emerges from the shadows. She addresses him as Pierre-François, a name he doesn't recognize, because since their first acquaintance, he has had occasion to use many pseudonyms. Lacenaire cultivates the look of a French dandy of the 1830s, with a stovepipe hat, ruffled shirt, long frock coat, walking stick, and black curls plastered to his forehead in a slightly absurd style. The dialogue by Jacques Prévert has an edge of menace, and it becomes clear that Garance isn't exactly pleased to see this old friend. He informs her that he has become famous, not as the writer he aspired to be, but as a criminal. They talk while facing a large mirror in which they see themselves reflected. He spins a tale as she plays with the glittering veil covering her gorgeous, impassive face. When she turns to take her leave of him, he grabs her by the arm and delivers some of the most beautiful lines in the film: "It's so painful to see you again, and find you unchanged. I'd prefer to find you ravaged, submissive, rendered stupid by wealth. Then I could have lived with an easy conscience, and my fine idea of mankind."

Kostrovisky said, "The subtitles don't capture the poetry of the words he spits at her."

I replied, "No. What a phrase: *crétinisée par l'argent*—cretinized by money."

He asked, "Would you like to meet for coffee some time?" I was caught off guard and said that would be fine. He wrote his phone number on the receipt and handed it to me. I passed him his tape beyond the security sensors, and he walked out. I locked the door after him and shut off the lights outside the store, then counted the cash in the register as *Children of Paradise* came to an end.

∞

The next day I woke up at ten a. m. I was scheduled to work another late shift, and I had no plans until four, so I puttered around the apartment, showered, and got dressed. I looked at the clock and noticed that it was barely lunchtime. The receipt with the number from the night before was on the telephone table across the room. That guy isn't even my type, I thought, but I'm bored and curious. During my years in Los Angeles, I'd found few people with whom I had much in common. I was able to get sex if I wanted it, but real conversation was a rarity for me. Perhaps this person would be someone with whom I could have the latter, if not the former. When I called, the voice on the other end of the line was bright and cheery. Either Kostrovisky was an early riser, or he was excited to hear from me. He suggested we meet at the Onyx at two p. m.

The Onyx, a coffee house on Vermont Avenue, was only a fifteen minute walk from my apartment, so I had no excuse to be late for our meeting, and yet I was. The place was perfectly pleasant, but I always felt reluctant to go there. For one thing, I didn't drink coffee, but there was something else, a suspicion that if I hung out at the Onyx, I'd be vulnerable to approaches from people I didn't really want to know. Whenever I walked by, which was often, I'd find a scene of wholesome industry: the people inside occupied themselves with writing or drawing. I came to the conclusion that they were really scribbling nonsense to hide how directionless their lives had become in Los Angeles's listless bohemia, baked a little too long in the California sun. Part of me knew that this prejudice was a reaction to my own lack of direction in life, but I couldn't justify paying for a beverage I didn't enjoy only to be surrounded by slackers.

Bernard stood up and waved as I walked in. We went to the counter, and he ordered a cappuccino for himself and an iced tea for me. As we settled into our chairs, I saw a book I didn't know on the table, *A Star-Bright Life* by Coleman Dowell. I asked about it, and he said, "My favorite novel of his is *Too Much Flesh and Jabez*. It's almost pornographic—a size queen fantasy and a chicken hawk fantasy, both narrated from the point of view of an old maid schoolteacher. I like this memoir, but it should be considered another form of fiction writing. The book's about as reliable as *Hollywood Babylon*. It's the story of a provincial *naif* who goes to New York to do something great. His youth, good looks, and guile lead to wretched exploitation by notable others. His aspiration was to write Broadway musicals, and he ended up writing experimental fiction instead, almost as an afterthought. There's something borderline mythomaniacal about him." At that point, I looked at the book again, and I noticed that I'd mistaken the title; it was actually called *A Star-Bright Lie*.

"Wow." I didn't know how to respond to such a neat summary of a life. "Is that the story of Bernard Kostrovisky, too?"

He let out a soundless laugh. With a mischievous glint in his eye, he said, "Call me Bernie." He cleared his throat and shifted his weight a little. I expected a brief autobiography, but instead he continued on the subject of Dowell. "A psychiatrist named Bertram Slaff was his partner and the anonymous patron who funded the publication of this book. He put up with a lot. Dowell would spend his days picking up homeless men in Central Park. I don't know if he had sex with them in their apartment, but he did jump off its balcony when he committed suicide. That made the news, briefly."

"How did you find out about him?"

"I used to spend a lot of time with the writer Marguerite Young, who was an acid-tongued gossip *par excellence*. She would refer to him only as '*that beast* Coleman Dowell,' without elaborating more than that, unfortunately. He published a story titled 'I Am the Beast,' so that may have been Marguerite's private joke with herself."

At the risk of putting Bernie on the spot, I decided to make a direct inquiry. "Where do you come from?"

"Detroit, more or less. I graduated from University of Michigan, then I went to New York. I got there in 1981, too late to snap up the dirt cheap real estate of the '70s."

"What did you do in New York?"

"I started out working at the Carnegie Cinema, which was a revival house tucked into Carnegie Hall and owned by a guy named Sid Geffen, whose business dealings were shady, to say the least. As difficult as those years were in some ways—I was new to New York, I knew no one, I was making just over minimum wage—they were remarkably colorful. Sid went through twenty-five managers in one year. *Children of Paradise* was a perennial favorite at that place. I think Sid must have owned a print of the film; the copy they always projected was in terrible shape. Since he didn't have to pay a rental fee to the distributor, it was almost pure profit."

I smiled and asked, "Do you know much about the film?"

"It was made partly in Vichy France and partly in Paris during the Nazi occupation. The star, Arletty, was tried for collaboration because she had an affair with a German officer during the war. She defended herself by saying, 'My heart is French, but my ass is international.' She was convicted."

I said, "I'm most curious about the Lacenaire character. He seems almost contemporary, wanting to become famous and take his revenge on the world."

"He's based on a real person."

"I didn't know that."

"He wasn't a very competent criminal, but he did dress like a dandy and fancied himself an author. I think he inspired Dostoevsky's *Crime and Punishment*. Anyway, one of his victims was a transvestite called 'Mademoiselle Madeleine.' I wouldn't be surprised if it was a crime of passion. The henchman in the film, Avril, looks at Lacenaire like he's in love with him, and I imagine this was based on fact, or at least hearsay. The actor who played Lacenaire was gay, to the bitter disappointment of one of the film's other stars, Maria Casarès. She developed an unrequited passion for him."

Bernie's story trailed off, and I asked, "What brought you to Los Angeles?"

"I'm at Cal Arts." He added sheepishly, "A sabbatical replacement for Allan Sekula, teaching History of Photography for a semester."

I looked over his shoulder at the clock and saw that I risked being late for work if we talked much more. "I need to get to Videoactive for an afternoon shift." I admitted, "I don't have a car. Can you drive me? It's a long walk from here."

"Sure, but I left my car parked at home. Do you mind walking as far as Ambrose?"

We headed north toward the area of Los Feliz that sloped gently upward to the hills of Griffith Park. The area had been a middle class neighborhood for as long as anyone could remember. The preferred style of its developers was Spanish colonial, what architecture critics used to call a "dishonest pastiche" that conferred a certain respectability, even during the recent economic recession that allowed a lower class element (including me) to move there. I had never walked down Bernie's street. I expected to pass the house

7

from *Double Indemnity*, but was surprised to see that he lived in an Art Deco building.

When he opened the door to his apartment, I saw a jumble of boxes and books. I asked, "How long have you lived here?"

"Oh, a while." He said in an offhand way, "Sorry, it's been the cleaning lady's day off for a few months now. I just need to find my car keys." As he fumbled around, I took in the view. I saw a bunch of photographs hanging on the far wall. Before I could get a good look at them, Bernie came back, keys in hand, and said, "Let's go." We went out to his car, a battered Ford Escort parked about a block away.

On the drive to Videoactive, I told him, "I'm sorry that was so brief. I didn't know what to expect. I don't normally see customers outside of work."

He said, "I understand. When I was a ticket taker at the Carnegie, I had to deal with lots of crazies. There was one guy—I wouldn't call what he did shadowing; it was way more noticeable than that. He used to follow me around. He became a running joke with the rest of the staff. 'Hey, that creepy guy was here asking about you,' et cetera. At that point in my life, I was downright catatonic and shy most of the time and didn't understand much, so I couldn't deal with this creature contorting himself in corners a few feet away from me on a fairly regular basis. I simply didn't react. What a strange time that was."

He finished his story as we pulled up to Videoactive. I kissed him on the cheek and said, "Thanks for the ride."

TWO

I didn't have to work the next day, and after waking up late, I decided to take a walk. I left my apartment near the Shakespeare Bridge, headed downhill toward Talmadge Street, then up a small hill to Hillhurst Avenue. At the corner of Franklin, I saw a southbound bus coming. Service was so infrequent on the route that I had almost come to believe it was a myth. I took the appearance of a bus as a sign that I should ride it to the end of the line. All of my fellow passengers were female: two older Korean women carrying packages and two young Latina women probably on their way to work. The pairs were involved in their own conversations and didn't acknowledge my presence.

I looked out the window as Hillhurst turned into Virgil on the way to the neighborhood that had been renamed Koreatown in the 1980s. Los Angeles was building a subway system—the sort of project that outsiders thought was a huge joke—and the excavation caused significant disruptions along Wilshire Boulevard, the proposed route. Its eastern reaches had fallen into disuse, and enterprising Korean investors, who saw an opportunity in white flight, were buying up real estate in areas that would one day be well served by public transit.

The Korean pair got off the bus where Virgil ends at Wilshire, while the three of us who remained took it to the route's terminus, the Westlake/MacArthur Park subway station near the corner of Seventh Street and Alvarado. As I stepped onto the sidewalk, I turned to look at the sign on the front of the bus, which said "26 Short Line." I'd have to catch it in the opposite direction to get home.

Just out of curiosity, I took the subway. I bought a round trip ticket for $2.00. I didn't have a lot of company. At one point, I was the only rider in the car. I couldn't blame people for staying away, because the system didn't really go anywhere. There were five stops, the last being Union Station. I got out of the train there and took a look around. I saw a couple of beautiful spaces to which the public had no access because the film industry used them for locations. I didn't want to take an Amtrak train and arrive at some far-flung destination hours late, or a commuter train and end up stranded in the suburbs, so I got on the subway again and headed back to Westlake.

When I reached the surface, I had no specific goal, and I wandered at the edge of MacArthur Park. I didn't go into the park, because I wasn't interested in buying drugs. The intersection of Alvarado and Wilshire was the center of another world, one that residents of my neighborhood tended to ignore, because immigrants lived there. I once read that 90057 had the highest population density of any US zip code, a remarkable statistic considering that there were very few high rise buildings in that part of the city. I didn't doubt it based on what I saw on the street. People were milling around everywhere, buying and selling all kinds of goods from cassette tapes to apparel, cooking, eating, listening to music, and trying to get from one place to another. On the few available seats, people were socializing or waiting for the next bus.

On a relatively quiet block near the park, I saw a large sign reading "Libros Revolución." I decided to find out if they sold English language books. I had visited another store like it in San Francisco, where I bought a copy of *Red Detachment of Women*. I had a weakness for communist countries' propaganda. I couldn't imagine how the original audiences understood those Technicolor revolutionary operas, with their extreme performances and garish color schemes, but to me they seemed saturated in camp.

What I encountered upon entering the store wasn't exactly chaotic, but it was certainly in transition. Shiny new cultural studies books were starting to replace publications covered in many years' accumulation of dust. The socialist governments of Eastern Europe were all long gone, and state publishing houses' editions of classic Karl Marx texts—always far cheaper than American academic books—sat neglected on the shelves. Yellowed portraits of Marx, Engels, and Lenin, along with somewhat brighter ones of Mao Zedong, Che Guevara, and Patrice Lumumba, occupied prominent places on the wall. I couldn't imagine how this retail environment would attract the people I had seen on the street. Even I didn't feel very comfortable in the midst of what looked like a rummage sale of world history.

I decided to approach a clerk, whom I expected would judge me harshly for my ironically trashy attire and impractical hairstyle. Ripped jeans and a bowling shirt hung off my skinny frame, and my hair was down to my shoulders. I was about to devise a snappy comeback to an anticipated insult when I recognized my old friend Moira sitting behind the counter. I saw her before she saw me, so I took a moment to observe how the last few years had treated her. The Moira I had known in college was rail thin, nearly six feet tall, with short platinum blonde hair. The person I saw in front of me was heavier, and her longish hair had started to go gray.

I cleared my throat, and she looked up at me. "Guillermito!" she exclaimed. I didn't know where to begin a conversation, but fortunately, she did it for me. "I was just wondering how I could reach you."

We hugged and I said, "I've been in the same apartment in Los Feliz for years."

"What brings you to this neighborhood?" she asked.

"I thought I'd ride the subway. A bit of an anticlimax."

"It's a terrible waste of money. They're diverting funds from the bus system to build it. And where will it go? The subway will never serve the population that needs public transportation the most." Her eyes narrowed as she looked at me. "You drove here?"

"No, I took the bus. I don't have a car anymore."

Moira shuffled through some papers and handed one to me. It was a flyer announcing a meeting of the Bus Riders' Union, a new organization pressuring the city to provide better public transit. She said, "I know you don't involve yourself in politics, but it's in your interest to join this group."

"Hey, I vote in every election."

She scoffed at me. I remembered her contempt for representative democracy, which she dismissed as hopelessly compromised. That made me think of her father, who was connected to city politics in some way I had never figured out. I asked, "How's your family?"

"I haven't spoken to them in a while." She didn't look happy to announce this, and I didn't want to dampen the mood by asking for more details. There was a brief silence, broken when someone came into the store.

"*¿Qué onda, blanca?*" asked a man who came up and kissed Moira on the cheek, making her blush slightly. The two of them immediately started talking in Spanish. I gathered that he also worked in the store, but their political activities were the main topic of conversation. I wasn't introduced to him, and he completely ignored me, so I moved behind a nearby bookshelf and leafed through a thirty year old copy of Marx's *Grundrisse*. It quickly became clear to me that Moira's friend didn't come from the same place as any of the immigrants in the neighborhood. He spoke in the rapid monotone of Mexico City. He rattled off acronyms and phrases I didn't understand. I assumed

Moira did, but it was impossible to tell. He hardly let her get a word in edgewise. His back was to me, so my main view was of his shapely ass. The sight of it in tight jeans made me reconsider my first impression that he was Moira's boyfriend. I imagined how his ass would look in motion while he walked, perhaps when cruising for rough trade in MacArthur Park. This reverie made me drop the book I had in my hands. The man looked over his shoulder the way someone would look at a servant who had just broken a piece of crockery. He asked, "¿A dónde se fue el flaco?"

I spoke up and said, "I'm over here, admiring your ass from a discreet distance."

Moira giggled as he gave us both a look of embarrassment and disdain. He muttered something, but the only word I could make out was *payaso* (clown). He turned to face me directly and stared for a moment. I took in his appearance. He was tall and pale and very handsome. He wore a polo shirt and had a three day beard that looked well cared for. He could easily have been a corporate lawyer on his day off. He looked me up and down, but he didn't pause at my crotch. Perhaps he was straight after all. Moira, sensing a potentially unpleasant confrontation, eased the tension by saying, "Temo works the next shift. I'll drive you home." She took my arm to lead me to the door.

As soon as we were out of earshot, I asked, "Who's Temo?"

"That's short for Cuauhtémoc." She rolled her eyes. "You two, I thought I was going to have to break up a pissing contest."

"If only." I asked, "What's his story?" To my mind, this question meant "Is he gay?" but Moira chose to take it literally.

"He's from Mexico City, and he's here to do a PhD in urban planning. He can be abrupt, but he's a good guy." We got into Moira's car, an old Honda with a weathered paint job. "I like working at the store. Temo and I are trying to update the stock, over the objections of the manager. He's a hardliner, but he realizes the collected writings of Stalin aren't going to be popular in Westlake.

He dismisses us as opportunists or fashion victims, but he has more of a sense of humor than I expected."

"He'd have to. A lot of the stock looks pretty anachronistic, to put it kindly."

Moira said wearily, "Oh, don't tell me you've bought into that neoconservative 'end of history' bullshit."

"Of course not. I actually love some of those old leftist books."

"You mean the ones with pictures." This remark was more or less true. She asked, "Do you want to have a cup of tea at my place?"

"That would be great." It was the first time she had let me see where she was living since we were in college, and I was pleased.

∞

Moira lived on a hill in a neighborhood that didn't have a name, since there was no homeowners' association trying to increase the value of their houses. The Hollywood Freeway cut the area off from Silverlake, which lay to the northeast. There was no reason to climb the hill unless it was to pay a visit to someone who lived there. Her apartment was large and airy and had a nice unimpeded view of downtown's skyline. It was close to many things on that side of town yet quiet. I wondered how long the neighborhood would remain neglected by real estate speculators.

The interior of Moira's apartment was austere in the extreme. I would have expected nothing less from the one college friend I could call an authentic leftist. Although we were very close in those days, we went our separate ways after graduation, and she disappeared for a while. During that period I worried about her safety, but I had no way of reaching her. Every so often she would call me, always from a different location and evasive about her activities. I was relieved to find her in a safe situation close to where I lived.

Over tea Moira and I caught up. Her life had been much more eventful than she let on, but I knew that if I got too inquisitive, she'd cut the conversation short. She told me that after a horrific stay in the war zones of Central America, she returned to her family in Hancock Park. Their attitude toward her political convictions quickly became intolerable, so she took the first remotely appropriate job she found and moved to a neighborhood only a few miles east of where she grew up. She had no regrets, because the comfortable, conventional life her parents wanted for her held no appeal.

I spoke about my life, but there wasn't much to tell. I had been working in a video store for a few years. I owned almost nothing and barely scraped by, but I valued my independence. I said, "When I'm not at Videoactive, I'm usually watching movies or writing."

Moira asked, "Anything you want to show me? Is it fiction or nonfiction?"

"I'd call it autobiographical fiction. You know, I change the names." I paused to consider how much I should tell Moira, then decided just to blurt it out. "A while ago, I started seeing a guy named Daniel. I would fist fuck him. The sex brought a lot of emotions to the surface. Daniel grew up in El Salvador, and he saw atrocities. It's a wonder he didn't go insane." I took a breath. "I got a vicarious glimpse of terrible things through his eyes. Our meetings were incredibly intense. The best way for me to make sense of it all was to start writing."

Moira asked, "Is Daniel your boyfriend?"

"No, but I'm the one person who understands him. I don't know how I can describe my role in his life. I needed to take a step back from the relationship. Daniel has no plans to leave his boyfriend, and I wouldn't ask him to. They're buying a house together, and they're both buying houses for their mothers. With all those mortgages to pay, there's not much time for me."

Moira asked, "Do you know the boyfriend?"

"Not really. He's from the former Soviet Union, and he sells real estate. He seems to care a lot about money. So does Daniel. They're immigrants. As an all-American Ivy League fuck up, I enjoy the luxury of not giving a shit. I grew up in a stable society, so I have a blind faith that everything will turn out okay. No one is going to behead members of my family because neighbors denounced them, and the currency isn't going to become worthless overnight, so I get to play at being a bohemian."

Moira said, "It doesn't have to be play."

"No, I suppose not. I'm finding my way."

"Aren't we all?" Moira's voice had a note of fatigue, which I read as an indication of doubt about her politics. She said, "I don't understand the world sometimes. I see so much suffering, and only callousness and corruption in response. I think a socialist revolution must be coming soon. It's the only rational solution. And yet lots of people in this country identify with the rich instead of the masses they exploit."

I said, "Maybe they're the gullible souls who believe they were Cleopatra in a past life, not the poor slaves who built the pyramids."

This made Moira laugh. She got up and said, "Before I forget, I have something for you." She went into another room and brought out a large box. I opened it and saw several illustrated Chinese revolutionary opera books, including my favorite, *Taking Tiger Mountain by Strategy*. The covers were slightly worn, and the prices were absurdly low. In response to a look of surprise on my face, Moira said, "We've been getting rid of books at the store. There's no distributor to return them to, and no archive will take them. Maybe you can use them."

"Thank you." I hadn't the slightest idea what I would do with her gift, but I gladly accepted it.

"I'll drive you home. I'm having a meeting here in a couple of hours," she said.

For the first time in years, Moira gave me her phone number. "I'll call you some time," I said as she dropped me off. She waited to make sure I got in the door with my ungainly burden.

THREE

The next day I worked a late shift, so I took the whole morning to look at what Moira had given me. Beneath several Chinese books, there was a picture book in Spanish, *Arte Zucheano*, about culture in North Korea. *Zuche* was the Spanish version of a word usually translated as "self-reliance" and transliterated as *Juche* in English. To my eyes, the still photos from theater and film productions looked similar to those in the Chinese books, all bright colors and heroic poses, but with more emphasis on traditional culture, which was appropriate for a country that had essentially been a colony for much of its modern history, until Kim Il-sung led Korea's liberation from the imperialists.

I called Bernie and told him about my new books. I figured he'd be interested as a collector, and might know more about them than the staff of Libros Revolución. His response was immediate. "Oh, wow. What's your address?"

He came right over and together we pored over the contents of the box. I was amazed to discover near the bottom of the pile a copy of *Forty Years of Socialist Albania*, published in 1984. At that time, only the Albanians rivaled the North Koreans in their combination of ideological severity, cult of personality, isolationism, and grinding poverty. From available evidence, it seemed likely that the citizens of the Democratic People's Republic of Korea believed wholeheartedly in the *Juche* idea and in the goodness and strength of Kim Jong-il, who a few years before had succeeded his father in the socialist world's only hereditary monarchy. I had my doubts about the Albanians. One look at the heavily retouched face of their leader Enver Hoxha made me wonder if the regime was a giant scam.

In the aftermath of World War II, Albania first allied itself with Yugoslavia, but in light of intelligence suggesting that Josip Tito wanted to annex Albania as a seventh Yugoslav republic, the focus shifted to befriending the Soviet Union. Hoxha worshiped Joseph Stalin, saw him as the true heir of Marxist-Leninism, and sought to emulate him. After his death, the USSR embarked on a period of de-Stalinization that was widely understood as a positive political development. Hoxha denounced it as revisionist treachery and broke off relations. He then approached the People's Republic of China just as it began the Great Proletarian Cultural Revolution, a calamity of immense proportions for everyone but Mao Zedong and his young followers who wanted to skip school and terrorize people. Although the outside world found the alliance bizarre, it served Albania reasonably well, at least until President Nixon's visit to Chairman Mao. Hoxha surmised correctly that when the Chinese entered into diplomatic relations and trade with the United States, they would have little use for him as a means to annoy the Soviet Union, or as anything else. Thus Albania, which depended almost entirely on foreign aid, was left without a friend in the world, its economy in ruins.

I picked up the last book in the trove that Moira had given me: *Enver Hoxha, His Life and Work*, published by Albania's Institute of Marxist-Leninist Studies in 1985, the year of his death. After an introductory panegyric by his successor, Ramiz Alia, Hoxha's life unfolds in pictures. I was drawn to a section devoted to his study abroad in France. Striking a rakish pose in a photo taken in

Montpellier in 1933, he was obviously quite the dandy. In every picture he's wearing a different suit. Somehow this Frenchified city slicker later became a partisan, living in the mountains and sporting a military uniform. The book represents this period with a grid of portraits of the founders of the National Liberation Councils as Organs of the Unity and Struggle of the Albanian People. Hoxha looks unbothered with his shirt unbuttoned, showing a bit of chest hair. The others look deadly serious. One man has a prominent gash on his cheek, which seems to sag slightly. Another has a bushy beard and resembles a Muslim cleric. I remembered that for many years, bearded foreign visitors were turned away at the border and could not enter Albania. This was a way of resisting the threat of Western individualists like Beatniks or hippies, though the sight of this man's picture made me think that outlawing beards was also a way for an officially atheist state to disavow its past as the only predominantly Muslim country in Europe. The woman of the group, Nexhmije Xhuglini, looks more like a schoolmarm than a revolutionary and gazes directly into the camera with a severe and pitiless expression. Soon after this portrait was taken, she married Enver Hoxha and became a source of strength for a dictator who was cultivated and rather soft compared to most communist leaders. The other men in the pictures would fall away from the narrative, presumably after having been purged. Nexhmije would endure.

After Enver Hoxha suffered a near-fatal heart attack in 1973, there was speculation that he stopped exercising absolute power and left the running of Albania mainly to his wife. This was the worst period in the troubled history of the country, which had become completely isolated. "Uncle Enver" paid little attention to the crisis, preferring to write thousands of pages of memoirs extolling the political line that had brought Albania to disaster. He was the most prolific author by far among heads of state, and his self-justifying mendacity knew no bounds. Cooped up in his villa scribbling away, Enver Hoxha invited comparisons to the Roman emperor Tiberius, who as an old man retired to Capri, where he indulged his most peculiar appetites. There were stories, told only in the strictest secrecy, that Hoxha had also become a crusty old pervert, victimizing a host of handsome young men.

Albanians themselves were often less informed than people abroad about what was really happening in their country, and as a result, wild rumors circulated: in the absence of legitimate economic activity, Albania had become a center of drug trafficking, a depot for the shipment of illegal arms, a haven for money laundering. No one could say if any of the stories were true, but they couldn't be proven false, either. All practical realities in Albania acquired the aspect of a dream, or more likely, a hallucination brought on by gnawing hunger. The only thing the great mass of Albanians knew with certainty was that they remained poor while the elite lived well. Soon after the socialist government fell, Nexhmije Hoxha was tried for embezzlement and imprisoned. She repeatedly asserted, "No money stuck to our fingers," but few believed her.

∞

I had researched the shifting political alliances in the socialist world when I briefly entertained the notion of writing a fantasy novel entitled *Stalin's Vagina*. In the book as I conceived it, Stalin was a hermaphrodite with oracular powers, experiencing visionary trances when squatting over the fuming vents of a seismic rift. This knowledge was kept absolutely secret, and anyone who suspected the true source of Stalin's power had to be eliminated. I was most interested in Stalin's early life, when he was a bank robber in the Caucasus, and his ready access to money earned the Bolsheviks' trust. Considering what he later became, he was also shockingly handsome. While on one of his escapades, or so I planned to write, he nearly succumbed to the vapors at an abandoned Zoroastrian fire temple in

Baku, where petroleum oozed from the ground and easily ignited. I envisioned the narrative as a communist version of *Myra Breckinridge*, but as I read more about the history of the Stalin era, my mood turned to despair, and I didn't feel remotely equal to the task.

∞

Bernie looked up from the book he had in his hands, a guide to art instruction during the Cultural Revolution, and asked, "Have you got *On the Art of Cinema* by Kim Jong-il?"

I answered, "I didn't see it in the box. Maybe it's still on the shelf at the store."

"That's a shame. Do you think he has good taste in films?"

I smiled. "Doesn't every dictator? They want to be movie stars."

"But the lack of a sense of humor doesn't help."

"Yeah, unlike Charlie Chaplin or Buster Keaton, they're all too afraid of falling on their asses."

Bernie responded, referring to a George Bush mishap in Japan, "I guess the benefit of living in a democracy is that we get to see the leader of the free world vomiting in public." We both laughed.

I said, "Growing up during the Cold War, I was curious about how people really lived under socialism. The Berlin Wall was built before I was born, so it seemed like it had always existed. I visited East Berlin in the 1980s. It was like a trip back to the '50s. I saw lots of unrepaired damage from the war, and lines of bullet holes at the level of human heads on the buildings in the center of the city. All of that's gone now, I'm sure."

Bernie said, "You were lucky. My first trip to Berlin was after the Wall came down, and the place had already changed a lot."

"West Berlin was totally fake, on financial life support from the Federal Republic of Germany and the Western Allies. The city was walled in, surrounded by the German Democratic Republic, which was propped up by subsidies from the USSR. Without them, the country's economy would have collapsed, which is exactly what started to happen in the early '80s. The Soviet Union needed foreign currency to save its own economy, so it sold oil to the West, and cut back the amount going to East Germany, which had no oil reserves, and had to mine coal to produce enough energy to meet its needs. The model satellite state choked on pollution and never made up the deficit."

"I didn't realize that."

I continued, "I'll never forget news footage I saw of the government celebrating the first microchip manufactured in East Germany. What was its capacity? One whole megabyte." I shook my head. "The events of 1989 were inevitable. Something was already taking its course. The only way socialism could succeed in Eastern Europe was by quarantining itself from the capitalist world. As soon as those countries allowed interactions with the West, the whole system went *kaput*. Besides, any society that builds a wall around itself is doomed, isn't it?"

We lost track of time while looking at these images of a lost world, and I was startled to see that my shift was about to begin. Fortunately, Bernie had driven to my place and was able to give me a ride to work. On the way, we didn't discuss what we'd spent the afternoon looking at. He kept his reactions to himself, though he was clearly as fascinated by the books as I was.

∞

I arrived at Videoactive and saw the manager, who didn't seem to notice that I was a little late. We talked for a while, and I made a suggestion for a new category in the gay porn section of the store: Eastern Europe. I had noticed that an increasing number of videos shot in the region were being distributed in the US, and from the reaction of certain customers, I knew that they had an enthusiastic following. In its extensive porn section, Videoactive assigned some of its categories to production companies like Falcon Video or Catalina, and others to directors like Joe Gage or Bob Jones (who, despite using his real name, had been successfully sued by a Christian university in the South); the rest were organized by fetishes, such as bondage and corporal punishment. In defense of my argument, I held up a copy of the recent video, *Men of the Balkans*. Its cover featured a handsome bit of trade with tattoos and a surly look on his face. According to the box cover, it was the first gay adult video shot in Bulgaria. I could only imagine the trouble the director, Jean Noël René Clair, took to make it. Performers had to be corralled, bribes paid, and moral panics averted. Intrigued, the manager grabbed the tape out of my hand and said, "Now that's pretty special."

"We're seeing a lot of them these days. I think they should be featured in the store."

"I'll take it home tonight, then," the manager said.

I blushed and admitted, "I already checked it out."

"Oh, for 'research,' I'm sure. Tell me how it is." He laughed as he left for the day.

After closing the store, I went home and put *Men of the Balkans* into the VCR. I also took out *Enver Hoxha, His Life and Work*. I looked first at one, then at the other while lying in bed. I quickly became sleepy. As I dozed off, I thought about how difficult it was to take advantage of free video rentals when I got home from work at eleven p. m. or midnight. I told Moira that I'd been writing, but it wasn't true. Standing behind a counter for eight hours a day and dealing with customers—some of whom found a special thrill in forcing me to put up with their personality disorders—left me with little energy to commit my thoughts, such as they were, to paper.

FOUR

After three rings, someone picked up the phone. "Hello?"

"Hey, Moira."

"How are you? I was thinking about calling you."

"I'm okay. I was wondering if you wanted to have dinner with one of my friends. He's seen the books you gave me, and I'm sure he'd like to meet you." I hadn't asked Bernie if this was the case, but I guessed that he'd be curious about my source.

"Of course." Moira asked slyly, "A new boyfriend?"

"No. How about Thursday night at Don Felix?"

"Let me look at my calendar." I heard her get up and walk across the room. "Yeah, that's fine."

"Let's say seven o'clock… um, do you want to bring Cuauhtémoc?"

"Why?" Moira sounded surprised.

"Oh, I thought you two were dating."

She got flustered for a moment. "Lots of people say that. We're comrades. I don't even know if he's straight."

I said, "All work and no play, huh? That ass of his is beautiful. It would be a shame if he didn't put it to use."

"*¡Ojalá que no!* You never quit, do you? Typical male."

"Oh, now don't be offended. I'm just kidding." After a pause I asked, "Does he ever talk about me?"

"Why would he? He's only met you once, and it didn't go well." Her tone changed. "You like him, don't you?"

"Well, I'm not sure he can even stand me."

"I confess I know nothing," Moira said in a tone so definite that I didn't feel like asking her anything more.

"See you Thursday at seven."

When I called Bernie and asked if he'd be interested in meeting Moira, he said he'd love to.

∞

Moira arrived late to dinner, even though the restaurant was only a short walk downhill from her place. "Sorry, I forgot the time," she said, offering no further explanation. It occurred to me that since she and Bernie might have little in common aside from their mutual friend, and I would be the main topic of conversation for the evening, a prospect that made me uncomfortable.

Perhaps rather foolishly, I ordered a Peruvian beer just because I liked the name, Cusqueña, and then another. I soon felt a stupor descending on me. As my friends talked, things seemed to be happening at one remove. Every so often, I'd contribute a word or two, but I felt I wasn't really the person saying these things, even if my mouth was moving.

Bernie asked Moira about her work in the bookstore, what Westlake was like, and if she felt safe there at night. Moira explained that she'd survived trips to battlefields, so a few drug addicts didn't strike her as much of a threat. She was tall and (as she put it) strange looking to the people in the neighborhood. The worst things she had to cope with were men staring and little children asking to touch her blonde hair. Bernie didn't bring up politics, but Moira couldn't help herself and talked a bit about revolution. Thinking this was an opportunity to draw me out, he asked my opinion.

I roused myself as best I could and said, "Why would I want a revolution? Society as it exists now allows me to revolt. Revolutions suppress individuality. They're all about the collective good, and they eventually become authoritarian. A one-party system, even if it's on the right side of history, so to speak, can't tolerate dissent. I know it sounds selfish, but I'd prefer the world *not* to change so that I can be against the world."

After a pause, Moira said with asperity, "Spoken like a true punk."

"I'm the product of decadent American individualism, but at least I'm being honest, with you and with myself." I was drunk by this point, and I couldn't believe I'd said something that made sense. It was the kind of statement I normally avoided if I wanted to keep peace with Moira, but the presence of Bernie restrained her from pointing out my errors at length.

I was grateful when Moira changed the subject and asked Bernie, "How are you liking Cal Arts?"

He said, "They pay visiting faculty really well compared to other art schools."

Moira said, "I've heard so many stories about the good old days: massive drug consumption, orgies in the daycare center, an animal sacrifice in a course about 'ritual.' It must have been total madness."

Bernie laughed silently and responded, "Well, nothing like that's going on now."

Moira said, "Things were wild there at one time."

I asked, "How do you know?"

She responded, "My cousin Al went to Cal Arts. He was in the Film School."

I looked at Moira. "You never told me that."

"I bet I did, dear. You probably weren't listening. Too busy fantasizing about Al." Moira told Bernie an abbreviated version of the story of her Cuban cousin, who came to the US in 1980 with the Mariel boatlift. His relatives in Miami paid for him to go to school. The arrangement worked well as long as they didn't find out he was shooting gay porn films every weekend with Cal Arts' camera equipment.

That last detail piqued Bernie's interest. "Did your cousin make any films I might have seen?"

"I'm not a consumer of pornography," Moira explained, "and I never thought to ask. Now I guess we'll never know, because he's… he passed away a few years ago." A look of sympathy passed between Moira and Bernie. Without anything being said, he knew that we were talking about AIDS. She continued, "It took us all by surprise, especially the more reactionary members of my family. They professed not to have known a thing, but Al didn't leave Cuba because he was a political prisoner." She thought for a moment. "I'm sure Al made his own films at Cal Arts, but I've never seen them. I think they were destroyed a while back. You know, to avoid a scandal." An angry expression crossed her face.

Bernie was suddenly intensely engaged in the conversation. "That happened to a lot of artists." He asked, "What was Al like?"

Moira said, "He was a perfect gay clone. In his family's eyes he looked like a typical Cuban *macho*. He was very charismatic, and I'm sure he got an enormous amount of sex. At the same time, his *machismo* inhibited him. He was a complicated guy. I don't think anyone really knew him." She looked up. "I've gotten a bit carried away. Sorry."

Bernie said, "No need to apologize. I lost someone recently. Did you know a photographer named Brian Weil?" Moira and I both shook our heads. "Well, he died in February, while I was out here." He looked down at his plate. "At least I got to attend the memorial."

"AIDS?" I asked.

"No, he died of a heroin overdose. The *New York Post* had a field day with the 'irony' that someone who advocated for IV drug users and their health was actually a user himself, as if that negated his position. I worked with him at the first needle exchange he set up in the South Bronx.

"He taught at the International Center of Photography, and I assisted him in his classes. He hated students coming late and he made a rule: if you were late more than two times you were kicked out of the class. One of the rich European kids there clashed with him constantly and came late to every class, so he told her she was kicked out. She began to scream at him, insisting she was going to stay. He pushed her out and slammed the door shut. When she tried to open the door again, he shouted, 'If you're not going to leave, I am!' He walked out and never came back. I finished teaching the class for the rest of the term. That was the beginning of my teaching career."

Moira asked, "Were you and he lovers?"

In response, Bernie stammered for a moment. He didn't address the question, but said, "Brian was extremely good looking and he had a nervous, slightly uncomfortable manner that accentuated how downright sexy he could be. He was also very funny. He liked to speak as lewdly as possible. He wanted a 'sidekick' in his classes, which is about how I'd describe my function there. I was very depressed in those days and seemed to give him impetus to describe all sorts of sexual scenarios involving me if we were discussing my photos with students. That was usually very entertaining and from Brian amounted to the highest praise possible." Bernie was in a kind of daze when he said this. "Not one but two boys, on two different occasions, two straight boys, did pictures of themselves jacking off for him. Maybe that's more common in photo classes than I realize, but at ICP there was a certain reserve about these things. Seeing it a second time made me think it wasn't a fluke. Brian had no boundaries, or at least that was what he wanted people to think. He could seduce anyone."

I asked, "Even you?"

He started muttering, "Well… um, I…"

To put an end to Bernie's misery, I asked him, "What was Brian's memorial like?"

Composing himself, he said, "It was in the Bronx and involved an afternoon of speakers. Like at a Quaker service, anyone could speak. He was an over-the-top personality and touched a lot of people's lives. His mother said, 'Brian always had a cause.' I heard quips like 'I knew him when he was gay,' which might have been a little surprising to his family, or maybe not. Brian would admit to everything, which could be even more opaque than saying nothing.

"Annie Philbin from the Drawing Center was there. Brian had been her lover at one time, I think. She has the language of a museum director that's grand and celebratory and in charge. It all sounds good. Anyway, she's moved on, dating Fran Lebowitz now. Fran, who probably didn't know Brian and was just there to support her girlfriend, must have been awfully bored. She left the long, long service several times for smoke breaks. It was noticeable because there were taps on her shoes that reverberated throughout the church." He raised his eyebrows and said in an antic voice, "Clickety-click."

Wide-eyed, Moira said, "What monstrous narcissism."

Bernie shrugged. "If you're not emotionally involved with someone, I don't know how monstrous it can be. Skilled narcissists make themselves interesting to other people. They're either amusing or tiresome."

"That sounds a little like something Oscar Wilde said once."

"Oh, he never said anything just *once*." We all laughed. "Besides, he died before the word 'narcissism' was used by anyone except a few psychiatrists."

I sighed, "Strange that there was a time before that word existed, since it has almost universal application today."

Moira turned to me and asked, "Speaking of making yourself interesting to other people, have you been writing lately?"

I protested, but the two of them ignored me.

Bernie grinned, and much relieved by the change of subject, said, "I knew there was more than meets the eye going on with you."

Moira added, "Yeah, the 'video store clerk' routine doesn't fool everyone, you know."

I said to her, "I haven't written anything lately, but I had an idea, inspired by all the books you gave me, and the porn I borrow from the store."

She said, "I don't see the connection, but I imagine you're onto something."

"I can't imagine anyone publishing it."

Moira said, "Your last piece of writing was about fist fucking, isn't that right?"

I blushed and nodded. "Yeah, an editor called it 'courageous,' which I now know is a euphemism for unpublishable."

Bernie chuckled to himself and said casually, "Maybe you should go to art school."

The idea immediately interested Moira, who said, "It would give you a way to escape Videoactive."

They both looked at me. I said, "Nothing like being put on the spot... um, don't I need a portfolio to do that?"

Bernie responded, "Sure, but if you can write a good essay, that's more than most art students can do. Believe me, I've seen some doozies in my time."

Moira said, "You can be the pornographer you've always wanted to be, you'll just do it at Cal Arts, following in Al's footsteps."

"All I can say is that I'll think about it." I rolled my eyes, but deep down I was intrigued. I had my doubts about being able to afford the tuition, but I said nothing.

Bernie looked at his watch and said, "It's getting late. I have a class to teach tomorrow. If you don't mind the detour, I can lend you a book that'll help you think about art school."

"That would be great."

The interior of Bernie's apartment was much the same as when I first saw it, perhaps a little messier. He started searching shelves and boxes for the book he wanted to lend me. I took the opportunity to look at the photographs he had hung on the walls. They were dark and strange and seemed to depict corpses. If I hadn't known Bernie, I would have been scared. I imagined that he didn't invite strangers home very often, if at all. I raised my voice and asked, "Whose pictures?"

Without me noticing, Bernie had come up behind me. He said quietly, "Brian Weil, of course." I nearly leapt with fright. He chuckled. "No cause for alarm." He said it with a hint of irony, as though he was reciting a line from an old movie. Bernie handed me a book, the exhibition catalogue *Helter Skelter: LA Art in the 1990s*. "You can borrow this. I know some of these people from school or seeing them around town."

We made our way through the maze of boxes to the door. Once we were outside, I could breathe more easily. The atmosphere inside Bernie's place was oppressive, but I was so transfixed by the disorder that I had hardly noticed. He dropped me off at home and I said, "Thanks for the book."

He responded, "Thank *you*. I hardly know anyone outside school. This is a tough city for socializing. I like Moira." I kissed him on the cheek and said good night.

∞

The next day I looked through *Helter Skelter*. It was an attractive but somewhat unreadable object, overly designed and expressing a sense of "cool" at every opportunity. The exhibition at the Museum of Contemporary Art closed on April 26, 1992, three days before the Los Angeles riots and nearly two years before the Northridge earthquake. These two events served as points of reference for every person living in Los Angeles. Named after Manson family crime scene graffiti intended to implicate the Black Panthers and start a race war, *Helter Skelter* struck a pose of bemused cynicism about the *noir* social landscape thriving in the shadows of palm trees. The breezily definitive subtitle of the book—*LA Art in the 1990s*—predicted the art world fashions of a decade that was only two years old when the show opened.

Helter Skelter reverses the order of a typical exhibition catalogue. Biographies of contributors are practically the first thing in the layout. The strategy has the function of legitimating the enterprise. In the table of contents, the artists and writers are listed as equals—a radical departure. I couldn't think of any other museum exhibition that presented visual art and creative (as opposed to art historical) writing together in its catalogue.

I read the capsule bios with great interest. Although only a handful of participants were Southern California natives, virtually all of them had connections to museums, universities, and art schools in the area. A glaring exception was Charles Bukowski, who had lived in Los Angeles since 1923 and belonged to an older generation that didn't have much use for institutional pedigrees. Most names were recognizable—the prediction of the exhibition was coming true—though the Hispanic participants, all but one of whom came from Los Angeles County, were less well known, an indication of the endemic racism of California. Ten held degrees from California Institute of the Arts, or its predecessor, Chouinard Art Institute. The number of participants with degrees from Yale or Cooper Union was zero. I attributed this to two factors: first, the boosterism inherent in MOCA's project, and second, the reluctance of alumni of prestigious East Coast art schools to deviate from an established path to success by making a perverse and foolhardy move to Los Angeles.

Like many people who saw the exhibition, I was strongly attracted to Mike Kelley's work. A lot had been made of Los Angeles artists' embrace of mass cultural materials—I was unsure whether they mined this subject matter any more enthusiastically than artists in other regions of media-saturated America—but Kelley's work had an extra dimension of pathos, because his sources were so resolutely proletarian. In *Helter Skelter*, he presented an installation prominently featuring his "Loading Dock Drawings," a series based on what he had found in the offices of Cal Arts' custodial and security staff. While a lot of his fellow graduate students were pondering the implications of Minimalism and debating the merits of Clement Greenberg, Kelley was paying attention to what the workers considered art. Crudely drawn and tasteless cartoons were enlarged to the size of an entire wall: a fish fellates a fisherman below the waterline; a boy and girl hold open their underwear and compare genitals ("Hey! Where's yours?"); and a man in a business suit appears next to the line, "If assholes could fly, this place would be an airport!"

The installation had been commissioned by Chiat-Day, an advertising agency with a building in Venice designed by Frank Gehry. Kelley's plan was to disturb the carefully maintained boundaries between the different classes working at the office by forcing executives to confront artifacts associated with janitors. (His father had worked as a maintenance man at a public school, and his mother had been a cook in a Ford Motor Company cafeteria.) This commission, canceled by its patrons, was reconstructed at MOCA, thus showing the work to many more people than would have seen it at Chiat-Day, but depriving it of its original social function. Kelley, who grew up in what Bernie called the "fetid downriver suburbs of Detroit," considered himself a blue collar anarchist. He summed up the attitudes toward culture in this environment when he said, "In my family, art was considered to be what communists and homosexuals did." If only that were true, I thought.

∞

A few days later, Bernie brought me an application to Cal Arts and I thanked him. That night as I fell asleep, I made the decision to apply to art school. I didn't know if it was due to the catalogue Bernie had lent me or to my loneliness (a constant in my life that I rarely reflected upon), but I suddenly wished to remove myself from my circumstances, in favor of a new environment full of people I had never met. I asked myself, Why not take a chance? I could think of no reason not to apply to art school, and none appeared to me in my dreams.

FIVE

The next few months passed quickly because I had a goal. I made an effort to go to art galleries, and I visited campuses. Otis College of Art and Design, at the edge of MacArthur Park, was the most convenient, as long as I caught the 26 Short Line bus, which became less enigmatic once I found a printed schedule at Union Station. I thought that when the Red Line reached Los Feliz— some time by the end of the 1990s—I'd be able to take the subway there. I found out during my visit that before this happened, Otis would be moving to a new campus in Westchester, near LAX. It was as though the school planned to flee from public transportation.

I went to Libros Revolución after Otis. I walked in and saw no one there. For an instant, I felt the urge to grab as many books as I could and run while no one was looking. I doubted such an old fashioned place had installed surveillance cameras—perhaps they objected to them on principle—but I didn't want to cause any problems for Moira, who had already provided me with free books. A moment later, I heard someone stirring in the store. A man wearing a Minutemen t-shirt and looking a bit flustered emerged from the back room. I walked over to him and asked for Moira, but he shook his head and mumbled that he didn't work there. He walked out of the store as he tucked in his shirt. After he left, I called, "Hello?" and suddenly Cuauhtémoc came out.

He frowned and asked, "What do you want, *payaso*?"

"I was just here to see Moira." As I said this, I looked at Cuauhtémoc more closely. He seemed uncharacteristically disheveled. His shirt was only half tucked in, and his fly was open. I looked in the direction of the door then back at him and said, "Sorry if I interrupted something."

This disarmed Cuauhtémoc, who said, "I can trust you not to tell Moira, right?"

"As long as you stop calling me *payaso*. Cute trick, by the way."

He shrugged and said, "Not bad. White guilt makes him a little too *mojigato* for me." I gave him a puzzled look. "Vanilla."

"Oh, right," I said. "But to be fair, there's not much you can do in the back room of a bookstore."

He smiled and said, "You'd be surprised."

"Nice." I smiled back.

"Moira is coming soon." He was staring at my crotch. "She told me about you."

I wasn't exactly sure what he meant by that, so I asked, "Fisting?" He nodded. I said, "Never had any complaints." I began to get an inconvenient erection. "Um, how long until Moira arrives?" I approached the counter to give him a chance to touch my hard cock. He knelt down.

Then suddenly from the front of the store we heard, "Temo?" It was Moira. If she had come in a few seconds later, we would have had some explaining to do. I grabbed a book from the counter and held it in front of my crotch. Cuauhtémoc stood and quickly zipped up his fly. He untucked his shirt rather than making the effort to finish tucking it in. I turned around, and Moira said, "My two favorite men are here at the same time. I hope you're getting along." She hugged me, and I kept the book where it was as our bodies pressed together. She gave me a funny look and asked, "What brings you to the neighborhood?"

"Oh, I've decided to look at art schools. I was at Otis this afternoon, but I heard the campus is moving to the airport."

"I know, that's a shame. Have you seen Cal Arts yet?" Moira asked.

"No, so far away."

"There's the Antelope Valley Line. When the earthquake destroyed the freeway, they built a bunch of new train stations very quickly."

"Maybe we can go up there together some time." I realized this was unlikely. Her car wasn't fit to drive over mountain passes.

"Have you been to UCLA?" asked Cuauhtémoc.

I said, "Yeah, but the graduate art studios moved off campus a few years ago. I didn't know that when I showed up."

"It's very hard to get in," he said.

I looked at him and said, "Thanks for reminding me." As Moira leafed through the day's mail on the counter, he took the opportunity to lick his lips lasciviously. I rubbed my crotch.

Moira, who noticed a tone of aggression in our voices but didn't see my gesture, said, "Behave yourselves, boys."

"I just came by to say hello. I should get going." Cuauhtémoc offered me a ride home, and I said, "Yes, please."

"Such a polite young man," he said to Moira. We both kissed her goodbye, then left the store and walked to his car, a new white Mazda Miata.

I spent the drive to my apartment looking at Cuauhtémoc. He was pale, with smooth clear skin marked by a pair of moles and a heavy black beard that he had taken great care to trim but not shave off entirely. He had remarkably thick hair combed into a style that resembled a pompadour. It appeared he'd never go bald. His eyes were dark brown and deep set, with a trace of a unibrow over them. I wondered if he ever plucked his eyebrows. Cuauhtémoc noticed me staring and asked, "How do I get to your place?"

"Turn right at Franklin."

As soon as we entered my apartment, I grabbed a nail file from the medicine cabinet and let him use the toilet. I busied myself with preparing my hands, spreading a few towels on the bed, and mixing a new batch of lube. He emerged from the bathroom naked. He had obviously been going to the gym, because he had only the faintest hint of a belly, though not the exaggerated pectoral muscles that most gay guys developed to impress other men, but which didn't impress me at all. He had very sturdy legs that were not as hairy as I expected. Most of his body hair ran from his pubes to his collarbone. I walked toward him, and I saw his brown uncut cock start to swell. I kissed him roughly and grabbed his ass. When I was finished, he said, "I don't kiss."

"You'll kiss me," I said seriously. "And your cock tells me you like it." I gestured past him and said, "The bed's over there." He followed directions, and without any prompting from me, got on all fours. I noticed a necklace with an image of the Virgin of Guadalupe. I reached out to touch it, and he firmly pulled my hand away to indicate that he wouldn't take it off. I turned and gazed at his ass. It looked even better without clothes. Most of it was naturally smooth, but his crack had a line of black hair, carefully trimmed. I didn't bother to take off my clothes and started massaging the hole with my lubed-up fingers.

"My pussy can take more than that," he said with his face buried in the pillow.

"Be careful what you wish for," I said as I slathered my hand with lube. I pressed my fist against his ass, and he let out a loud moan. His hole started to swallow it without much preparation. The Minutemen fan must have loosened him up at Libros Revolución, I thought. Once my full fist made it inside his rectum, he started breathing heavily. "Are you okay?" I asked.

He said only one word: "Poppers." I had a bottle at the side of the bed within reach of my left hand, so I didn't have to remove my right one from his ass. He grabbed the bottle and inhaled deeply, then a minute later said, "Now."

I noticed a dramatic dilation of his rectum and took it as a sign that I should start punch fisting him. I couldn't believe how quickly things were progressing. I plunged my fist into him at a considerable depth (half my forearm) and drew it out over and over, until Cuauhtémoc began to tremble in a way that made me think he might be having a convulsion. I stopped moving and left my fist inside him. His rectum closed tightly around it. Sounding like a weightlifter in competition, he let out a gruff exhalation. His whole body shook. Then he whimpered like a child, and another spasm seized him. When he calmed down, I took my fist out, and he screamed into my pillow. He stayed very still and continued to have spasms for several minutes. This fisting session had been one of the quickest and most intense I had ever experienced. I wondered if this was how he always acted on a first date. I stared into his hole. I could make out the movements of his colon. I was amazed at the gape. I wished I had kept a flashlight by the bed. I suddenly remembered that I needed to piss, but I didn't want to leave the bed. I unbuttoned my fly and pissed inside him just before his hole closed up.

I knew Cuauhtémoc wouldn't be able to hold my piss for very long, so I patted his ass and said, 'Let's take a shower." I quickly stripped and grabbed towels for us. He had such control over his sphincter that he didn't spill a drop of urine on the way to the bathroom. We got in the shower together, and I squatted down behind him to get a good view of his ass. I worked my fingers into his hole. As he relaxed, piss poured down on my hand. I fisted him until nothing more came out of his ass. I rose to see him smiling.

I turned on the water, which took a little while to warm up. He trembled in the cold. We soaped up and scrubbed the lube off our various body parts. We both got hard and jerked off together. He came right away, and I used his cum as lube. He knelt down, and

I ejaculated all over his chest hair. We rinsed off, dried each other's bodies, then dressed in silence.

Cuauhtémoc started to leave, and on his way to the door, he saw the box of books Moira had given me. He asked, "Do you like them?"

"Yes," I said, "but maybe not in the same way Moira does."

"I'll bring you more. Same time next week?"

I said quickly, "Yes, please." He smiled. I gazed intently into his eyes and asked, "So you enjoyed yourself?"

"Don't be stupid. A lot. But I don't like to talk about sex. That's for girls." A look of contempt briefly crossed his face. His eyes narrowed and he made sure I was listening carefully. "You can do anything you want to me, no limits. Don't ask, just do it. Understand?"

"No safe word?"

"Why? I can tell you know what you're doing, *flaco*. Don't be a coward." He opened the door and said, "Call me Temo."

As he started to leave, I called out, "Hey, Temo." He turned around. I drew closer to him and kissed him passionately on the lips. He kissed me back.

He said, "You're turning me into a faggot." I laughed at this, because I thought he was joking. He suddenly looked very serious and said, "You can fist me like a crazy fucker, but don't laugh at me. *That's* my limit." I nodded as I held back a smile. "Next week, I come to you. Don't go to Libros Revolución anymore. Moira knows nothing. No one knows anything. That's how I like it." And then he left.

∞

Every Thursday, Temo would come to my place at five p. m. to get fisted, always dropping off a book or two from Libros Revolución. He barely spoke during our time together, so I wasn't aware of how these books were leaving the store. I sometimes wondered if he stole them off the shelves in order to bribe me to have regular sex with him. Perhaps finding a skillful partner who wasn't going to do physical harm or play psychological games—the latter seemed to be more of a concern for him—was exceedingly difficult. Often when I made a tender gesture, Temo flinched. He preferred to be brutalized. He never expressed any willingness to discuss how he came to be this way, nor any recognition that he was different from the great mass of "normal" people.

∞

The books Temo gave me contained images of hope and progress. Nothing negative or critical appeared in their pages, unless it related to a pre-revolutionary reality. They told a story of utopia, literally "no place," and expressed a profound wish: that human beings and the societies they formed could be perfected, and deprivation, material and spiritual, could be banished forever. Actually existing socialism didn't turn out that way at all, as everyone noticed eventually. To hide the disparity between utopia and real life, socialist states manufactured their own realities. Their heroic propaganda had an erotic dimension never officially acknowledged, and consequently, these peculiar images, which nearly everyone preferred to forget, were irresistibly attractive to me.

As far as I could determine, this particular perversion of mine had its origins in childhood. I grew up in a place where most of the working class came from Eastern Europe. The descendants of serfs, they would have become model socialist citizens had their ancestors never left their native countries. Instead, they came to America, worked on assembly lines at Ford or General Motors, bought houses in the suburbs, and grew sedentary in their middle class prosperity. They pursued a capitalist utopia—in its way just as phantasmatic as the socialist one—made possible by an economy that started collapsing in the early 1970s. They and their children after them were betrayed, and they sought consolation in reactionary politics, an outcome convenient for the elites that used them and held them in contempt. I escaped this grim reality, but I missed the men who were enmeshed in it. I saw images worth fetishizing in the absurd excesses of propaganda, even though a socialist utopia bore about as much resemblance to my own life as the surface of the moon.

Over the next few weeks, I borrowed a big stack of videos shot in Eastern Europe. I started watching them to figure out what they had in common. I noticed right away that the performers, who had little or no exposure to Western gay porn, constantly looked at the camera. There were many expressions of hostility. I imagined an atmosphere of coercion pervaded the productions, though I had no way of knowing for sure, because I had never visited a set. I began taking notes on the videos—dates and places of production, companies and directors—with a view to making a video of my own.

The world I saw in Eastern European porn was the exact opposite of utopia. There was an almost unbearable pathos in the faces of some of the performers. I could only guess what their looks meant and what these young men were searching for. I didn't have the means to travel and interview the boy prostitutes of Prague or Moscow or any of the other cities of the East. I had to make do with what I saw in the movies they made, material which was fascinating but ultimately rather opaque.

∞

I decided that the first step toward making a video would be copying potentially useful excerpts of the sources. For that task I'd need a second VCR, which I figured I could borrow from Moira. When I asked her, she said, "Of course. I can bring it to you some evening, but not tonight."

"Thanks. Do you have a meeting?" As soon as I said this, I realized that even if she did, she wouldn't talk about it on her phone line, which she was convinced had been bugged.

"Actually, no." She sounded excited. "I'm meeting Temo's parents in a little while."

I was nonplussed. I asked, "Are you two dating?'

"Not exactly." She tried to sound casual, but it was obvious that she had developed feelings for her coworker, and I came to the unappetizing conclusion that he was exploiting them. "I can't figure him out, but a part of me is hopeful." I immediately understood why I wasn't allowed to come into the store. Moira was Temo's beard, and he hadn't let her in on the precise nature of the deceit. I didn't know him well enough to say whether this was a cynical ruse or something less conscious and sadder. I could hardly imagine Temo playing out a drama of heterosexuality, but maybe he actually believed it on some level. I had heard of fisting bottoms who considered themselves straight, happily married to women while enjoying all manner of large objects (cocks, dildos, even arms) inserted into their asses by strangers, unbeknownst to their families. Perhaps it was merely a particular sensation that they craved. Once an older woman at a bar told me that she had had a long term affair with a straight LAPD officer who liked nothing more than getting fisted by her.

One Thursday, I pressed Temo on these questions, and he exploded with rage. He looked like someone possessed, and delivered an impassioned speech: "As long as I live, I will never understand the American obsession with labels. You think by saying 'I'm gay,' you can explain your whole personality. You flee to the nearest metropolis to find others who have given themselves the same pathetic label. Then members of the 'community' finally discover that this three letter word is inadequate to describe the full range of human experiences. So you form splinter groups, each with its own language, until the 'queer nation' becomes so atomized, so alienated, that its citizens can't even have conversations with each other. Everyone is afraid of transgressing idiotic rules that are always shifting and never consistent. The person who violates them in the presence of some self-righteous piece of shit will be instantly ostracized. All because of semantics. I have news for the so-called community: these arguments are never going to win a political victory, and they're not going to get you laid, either. I think the people who take the moral high ground at all times and want to prove they are more oppressed than their neighbors are as dried up as old mummies. I want to tell them, join the priesthood, because then you'll really achieve something, like helping the sick and the poor. But no, you'd rather complain. Your politics are as bankrupt as your enemy's. When you become your fathers, impotent alcoholic wrecks who wonder where the years have gone, don't come crying to me. Hypocrites!" I listened to him with a sense of awe. At the moment he uttered the word "hypocrites," he looked like Jesus in Pasolini's film *The Gospel According to Matthew*. I had no idea where this anger came from, but I found it very arousing. When he finished his tirade, I flipped him over and wrecked his ass as I had never done before.

∞

Moira and I arranged to meet on Saturday, when neither of us had to work. I went to Circuit City on Sunset to buy RCA cables and blank VHS tapes. Before Moira was due to arrive at my place, I borrowed the most titles I'd ever checked out from Videoactive. The manager happened to be working, and he found this hilarious. As I left, he said, "Good luck with the 'research.' Remember they're all due by closing tomorrow."

I arrived back home just in time. It occurred to me at the last minute that I should hide my ever-expanding library of communist propaganda. If Temo was keeping one secret from Moira, he very likely kept others. She walked in with her VCR and said, "I like what you've done with the place," giggling.

"I could say the same to you," I said as I took the deck from her. It was difficult to tell whose apartment was more spartan. "Thanks very much for this. I'll have to mention you in the credits of the video, if I ever figure out a way to make them." I asked her, "How was meeting the parents?"

"They are *so* bourgeois. They live above Sunset Plaza part of the year. They have a place in Mexico City, too, and another somewhere in the countryside. Temo warned me not to talk about politics with his parents, and he wasn't kidding. When his dad started singing the praises of Francisco Franco, I excused myself to go to the bathroom."

After a pause I said, "I thought you were a little bit in love with that guy."

Moira blushed and burst out laughing. "He's handsome, I'll say that for him. But I'm sure he plays for your team. I might have considered dating him when we first met, but that's out of the question now. The worst thing is he's the biggest mama's boy I've ever met. His mother cut his meat for him at dinner like he's helpless. Whatever man or woman lives with him will be doomed to a life of servitude."

What Moira told me was at once stranger and more banal than I had imagined. I never expected Temo to invite me out to dinner after getting fisted, no matter how much he had starved himself beforehand. I assumed this was because he didn't want to be seen in public with me, but in fact dinner was always waiting for him at home with his parents. I was relieved that at least he'd never asked me to cut his food for him.

∞

I continued to see Temo every Thursday. I didn't have his phone number, and he never called me from home, only from the store, to confirm our meetings a couple of hours before he left work. I was amazed at his cleanliness, which I attributed to strict fasting and ingenuity in a cramped bookstore rest room. Our arrangement reminded me of how radical political cells worked: no meetings fixed far in advance, the next one arranged only at the end of the last, and nothing important communicated over the telephone. Anyone who didn't know about future meetings was excluded from the group. But Temo didn't abandon me; if anything, he was becoming more dependent on our time together.

Temo let me do whatever I wanted to him, as long as I avoided leaving marks on his face or hands, the parts of his body he couldn't hide from his parents. I had no problem with that limit. I pissed in his ass regularly, and I also made him drink my piss. I ate his ass and kissed him afterwards. (This was so "dirty" in his mind that he didn't express his usual complaints about kissing.) At some point, I started to fuck him without a condom, but I always pulled out at the last second, putting my cock in his mouth and making him swallow my cum. I also jerked off inside his ass, because his gape was so wide that both my cock and a hand fit inside it. Most men would have discussed and negotiated every one of these sex acts, but not Temo. He never once stopped me or expressed an objection.

One day, as he was on his way out the door, I asked him, "Do you know anyone who can edit video for me?"

"I'll tell you next week, okay?"

"Thanks."

∞

As promised, a week later Temo gave me a number to call. I didn't know whether this guy was willing to work for free out of the goodness of his heart, if Temo paid him, or if there was some sort of sexual barter going on between them. I wasn't naïve enough to think that I was Temo's only sex partner.

This man edited my material, and in addition to a three-quarter inch video original, he made several VHS copies. He also typed simple titles for me on a computer, just my name and date at the end, plus at the beginning, the name of the video, which was the last thing to be decided. I chose *Faces of the Balkans*, a variation on *Men of the Balkans*, the movie that inspired me. My video was a simple compilation of close ups of performers looking into the camera in Eastern European gay porn. I used the sound on the tapes "as found," mixed to equalize the levels, but otherwise unaltered. The running time ended up being four minutes. The cumulative effect of all these faces looking hostile or disgusted, asking for direction, or perhaps even pleading for help, was overwhelming.

I began to write an essay about the video. Despite the lack of reliable information at my disposal, I was able, based on the internal evidence of the tapes, to write at length about this new genre of gay porn. I proposed a thesis that I'd never heard or read before. Traditionally, sex tourism involved white people from rich countries fucking the people of the Third World. It almost never involved sex with poor white people. There were two major exceptions: Germany between 1919 and 1933, and Eastern Europe after the fall of communism. This departure from the norm in the first instance was a prelude to fascism. It looked as though fascism was a distinct possibility in the second instance as well, though this was still an open question, and subject to national or regional variations.

When poor white people suddenly found themselves treated the way people who are not white have always been treated, they took this to be an outrageous humiliation. The result was a recrudescence of racist, nationalist politics. I took care not to impute a strict cause and effect relationship to this phenomenon, because, as I saw it, hyperinflation, economic depression, and mass unemployment were the main determining factors. Nevertheless, I was amazed to see a social transformation recorded in pornography. Such material had not been studied seriously because it was widely seen to be beneath scholars' consideration, but to me, this made it more appropriate as an object of historical analysis than masterpieces of film art, with their insinuating rhetoric and latitude for personal expression.

I wondered what would have happened if Christopher Isherwood had brought a movie camera rather than a notebook to Berlin and made porn films with his working class sex partners. He claimed a camera-like objectivity for himself, yet he didn't record the details of his sex tourism, because he occasionally formed sentimental attachments to the boys. It was precisely this romantic quality that appealed to those who flocked to adaptations of his *Berlin Stories*: the play *I Am a Camera* and the musical *Cabaret*, both of which were made into movies. One night, I borrowed *Cabaret* from Videoactive. I enjoyed the musical numbers, but the script that connected them seemed to have been one long exercise in dissembling. I preferred *Men of the Balkans*. I only wished there had been a *Men of Berlin*, produced circa 1930 and somehow surviving the depredations of fascism and the war. I appreciated the prodigious talents of Liza Minnelli and Joel Grey, but I would rather have seen a varicose vein on a Bulgarian's foreskin than a fictionalized Christopher Isherwood miming heterosexuality.

∞

A month or so after finishing the video *Faces of the Balkans*, I received an acceptance letter from Cal Arts. I called Bernie to let him know. He responded, "That's great."

"I thought I should tell you first since it's your fault."

"I hope you don't feel that way."

"No, but it *is* expensive," I said. "I'll be going into debt, and I've already got a bankruptcy on my record."

He said, "Lots of people have those nowadays. I think it'll be worth it."

I told him about the video I had submitted with my application. I could hear him laughing quietly on the other end of the line. I told him, "It's a crude piece of video art, but it must have interested the people looking at my portfolio."

"Cal Arts likes artists who have good ideas, and they don't care so much about technical accomplishments. They tend to admit people who wouldn't be accepted anywhere else."

"Is it as bad as all that?" I asked.

"I think that's their strength. Students have gotten so professional these days." There was a note of contempt in his voice when he said the word "professional." He continued, "I only taught there one semester, but I saw a lot. Take advantage of the place. Some students are only there to find themselves, and what they find is that they aren't really artists. Others are there just to look cool and hang out. They usually get into drugs. A few work very hard, and they're the ones who do well."

He asked me if I was going to commute, and I replied, "Moira told me that some art students live in their studios. I can't really afford to do anything else."

"Yeah, they do, but you have to be careful." There was a pause. He said, "Call me whenever you want. I won't show up on campus, since I'm not working there anymore, but maybe we can meet downtown if you take the train."

"I'd like that."

"Don't be a stranger."

SIX

Registration at Cal Arts was pandemonium, a scramble to sign up for classes with all the students and faculty present in the largest space on campus, the Main Gallery. State schools had switched to computerized systems, but at Cal Arts, all of this business was conducted in person, as though everyone was constantly auditioning. A mood of anxiety hung in the air. Since hundreds of people were involved in the process, and they were all speaking at once, there was an unbelievable din, and I had to yell to be heard by some of the older faculty members. I arrived near the end of the day, because it had taken the better part of the afternoon on public transportation to reach the campus in the distant suburb of Santa Clarita. By the time I approached the tables where students lined up to talk to faculty or their assistants, some courses were already fully enrolled. I saw a couple of tearful scenes. I managed to fill my schedule with less popular offerings, but I did get a place in Post Studio Art. This course, taught by John Baldessari the first semester the Art School held classes, had become a perennial Cal Arts institution. No one could give me a precise definition of "post studio art," but the course was universally understood on campus as a rite of passage.

I attended the Art School's orientation meeting at the end of the afternoon, and I got a first look at my fellow students. Most were dressed in thrift store clothes and struck slovenly and bored poses, playing down whatever excitement they felt at the prospect of starting a master's degree. A few looked eager, because they had come from another culture, either a foreign country or an educational background that didn't include art school. I started to doze off during the meeting but woke up when one student asked about the possibility of living in his studio to save money. The question got dismissed, but then in a stage whisper, the studio manager said, "It's our legal obligation to deny this happens. We can talk after the meeting." I decided to stick around.

The loan refund check I received seemed like a lot of money, but when I started to calculate my expenses, I realized that with a work study job (which paid very poorly) I wouldn't be able to afford my apartment, even if I found a practical way to commute. A few others had come to the same conclusion, and these students stayed to hear about the unwritten rules of studio living. Futons and hot plates were fine, as long as they could be hidden when the fire marshal made inspections once each semester. Campus security was aware that students often slept overnight in their studios and looked the other way as long as students didn't call attention to their semi-permanent residence.

The conversation turned to other topics that were of less interest to me, and my attention drifted. I began to look more closely at the people who would be my neighbors in the coming weeks. I noticed an attractive guy in the group. He hadn't said a word, and we weren't in a situation where our names were called, so I could only guess who he was from the way he looked. Appearances could deceive, especially in art school, but outwardly, he seemed to be exactly the sort of person I wanted to know. He had black hair cropped short and a beard so heavy that he must have had five o'clock shadow by noon. His face was rather pale with Mediterranean features that I found very pretty. A scar interrupted his left eyebrow and spoiled the symmetry of his face. I imagined that he had been the sensitive boy of his family until he became an anarchist. He wore a black t-shirt emblazoned with a large letter A in a circle, and over it, a faded denim jacket. I couldn't see anything below his waist until he abruptly got up to leave. The door shut behind him with a loud slam. I waited a beat then got up from my chair, a metal monstrosity that made my legs fall asleep within minutes. I tried to leave as casually as I could, but if anyone had cared to notice, my pursuit would have been obvious. I went out the door and looked left and right. He was nowhere to be seen. Perhaps he disappeared behind one of many nondescript doors punctuating the long hallways of the building.

I wandered around for a while and got lost. I wanted to take a look at the facilities, and after some effort, I found my way to the Annex building, where most of the first year MFA students would have their studios. The doors were locked. Outside I saw a guy smoking. At first glance he looked completely normal, or someone's idea of normal after being bombarded with a steady diet of Abercrombie and Fitch advertisements. He had short brown hair parted on the side, horn-rimmed glasses, and wore a long sleeve shirt with a button-down collar. His jeans had the dark color of a recent purchase, with the bottom precisely cuffed. He wore penny loafers with actual pennies in them and no socks. My first impression was that a nostalgic lifestyle spread from the *New York Times Magazine* had magically come to life. He asked me, "Do you have a key?"

"No," I said. "I thought maybe you'd have one."

"What a bore. I was trying to extricate a box stored in there." He stubbed out his cigarette. "Items of sentimental value and all that." His tone was a campy mixture William F. Buckley and W. C. Fields.

To make conversation I asked, "Are you from the East Coast?"

"No, Lompoc."

"As in *The Bank Dick*... a very fine film," I said with a smirk. "By the way, the outfit is working."

He laughed and asked, "Do you want to go for a ride in my vintage convertible?"

"Actually, I was hoping to get a lift home, but I wasn't sure how to find one."

"Look no further, young man."

I said, "I'm in Los Feliz. I hope that's not a bother."

He responded, "You're on my way. I live at the ragged edge of Koreatown, or the classy end of Westlake, depending on how you look at it. Have you heard of the Bryson Building?"

"I saw it in *The Grifters*, but I haven't been inside."

"No junky tricks for you," he said with a sidelong glance as he caressed his pomaded hair.

"I guess I haven't lived."

He pulled himself upright. "You're missing nothing. My fellow tenants are vermin."

His car, someone's idea of luxury in the late-1970s, was in perfect condition. He put the top down. I had never been on a Southern California freeway in a convertible. It was too late in the day to risk a sunburn, but I did take the precaution of putting a band around my hair. The car took a while to get up to speed on I-5, and he chuckled as other drivers blew their horns and passed him. On the way south, he made a detour by way of the truck route. "This old boat can't handle the mountain passes," he yelled while we were in a tunnel. "Besides, I have to urinate."

He pulled over at a rest stop. He parked the car and said, "I'll be back soon," with a smile.

I shielded my eyes from the setting sun as I inspected some papers I had been given at Cal Arts. After a while, I was bored and thirsty, so I got out and looked for a drinking fountain. I drank my fill of water and thought I'd take a piss, too. Once inside the men's room, I immediately saw what had drawn my companion to the place. Two men at the urinals turned their heads to see if I was a cop, and as soon as they noticed my long hair, they swiveled around to show their hard-ons. One was clearly a trucker, a slightly pudgy Latino man with a large brown uncut cock. He rolled his foreskin up and down and licked his lips. The other, a white guy skinnier and older than I, did the same thing without the foreskin. It's a shame they can't just jerk each other off, I thought, and then I revised my appraisal of the situation: they were looking for a three-way. I wasn't in the mood for that adventure, so I went to a urinal at some distance from them and pissed. When I'd finished and was at the sink discovering that the taps didn't work, I saw my companion walk by in the cloudy, graffiti-covered mirror. I followed him out the door.

"Did you enjoy that?" he asked as we both got in the car.

"I only took a piss."

"A shame. It's a good tearoom, especially at dusk." He looked in the rear view mirror and put his hair back in place. It had barely moved while he drove on the freeway with the top down, so I concluded that his activities at the rest stop must have been rather vigorous. "The trade is great today. Fridays are always the best."

"Is this the only rest stop in the area?"

"Oh, there's a wonderful one near Camp Pendleton, though that's a bit distant. Fellows are walking around with hard cocks tucked down their pants around there, simply aching for relief. You can get a half a dozen men in an afternoon without even trying, and some of them will invite you into their trucks. So much safer than getting fucked in a stall."

"As long as they're not psycho killers," I offered.

"I have a sixth sense," he said, pointing at his temple. "No gay knocks for me, Ida." I was a little taken aback that he was calling me "Ida," but I realized almost instantly that he was quoting the film *Female Trouble*. At that moment, he let out a gasp as a man passed our car. He drew close to me and whispered in my ear, "Take a look. That guy has a fucking elephant trunk for a penis. Magnificent."

I looked back at him and nodded approvingly. I asked, "Do you see many Marines at the Camp Pendleton tearoom?"

"I see 'em, but I never get fucked by 'em. They're all bottoms," he said with a resigned look.

"I guess they're used to being told what to do. Their asses must be works of art," I said.

"You've obviously done your homework. I don't go in for that, as you can tell. Give me a horny Mexican truck driver headed for the border any day. As long as he hasn't done a lot of speed, he can get it up and fuck the living daylights out of me, and be home in time for dinner with the wife and kids." He paused to savor that fantasy. "By the way, what do you get into?"

"I like fist fucking."

"In that getup?" He scrutinized my clothing. "You look like a mourner at Kurt Cobain's funeral. I thought it was all leather and hankies for you guys."

"I get away with it because I'm young. And give me a break, that leather stuff is expensive. If you have the skills, you don't need a costume."

"Well, you told me, now didn't you?" He glanced at his watch. "Jesus H. Christ, look at the time. We should get out of here before I get waylaid by another compelling member." He adjusted his mirror, started the car, and soon we were speeding down the freeway again. I would have been happy to talk more with him, but the wind and traffic noise were so loud that conversation was impossible.

As we pulled up to my apartment, he said, "You know, it's nice to meet someone at Cal Arts who's real."

"I'm not sure I know what you mean."

He snorted quietly and said, "You'll find out soon enough."

There was a pause. I asked him, "Have you ever been arrested in a tearoom?"

He smoothed his hair, looked around to see if anyone was listening, and said with a drawl, "Such close calls, you've no idea. One of my friends was nabbed by Lily Law in Echo Park, and to this day, he has trouble at immigration every time he's coming back into the country from abroad." He let this unpleasant story drop and said brightly, "Land sakes, I forgot to tell you my name. I'm Paul, like the great villain of the New Testament." I shook his hand. "By the way, don't believe all the stories you hear about me." He winked. "Only the raunchiest ones are true."

"Got a phone number?"

"Um, I don't have a pen and paper at hand. But fear not, you'll see me again."

I said, "Well, thanks for the ride. You're a life saver."

"No problem." He asked, "How the hell are you going to commute, anyway?"

"I'm giving this place up. I'll live in my studio."

"A shame. The train to Santa Clarita is so… invigorating." He got a faraway look in his eye. "The Methalope Valley Line has the roughest guys. They get out of jail or finish with a court date then walk to Union Station. Metrolink takes them back home to Palmdale or Lancaster. Simply amazing. But that's another tale for another time. I must be off."

"See you around, then." As soon as I got back into my apartment, I realized that I'd forgotten to tell Paul my name.

∞

On the first day of classes, I went wandering around campus and ended up at the studios again. Most of them were empty, but one showed signs of life. I heard music blaring through the door. I could make out the lyrics: "I am Damo Suzuki!" I approached to listen more closely. I knocked when the song was over.

The occupant of the studio came to the door and asked, "Is it too loud?"

"It's The Fall. Not loud enough."

She motioned for me to come in, and while she turned down the music, I took a good look at the place. The studio was much taller than it was wide, and a skylight in the roof illuminated the space. A large expanse of canvas took up the wall opposite the door from end to end—it was shaping up to be a painting of a woman's head. The other uninterrupted walls were full of smaller paintings and drawings and various accidental marks. The wall behind me as I entered had a small window, under which there was a table strewn with a huge pile of papers, and mixed in, audio cassettes and a tape player splattered with paint. There was a high table in the center of the room positioned near the painting in progress. It served as a large palette with an array of colors spread around a glass surface. The occupant of the studio didn't seem to mind me staring. She had an appearance I could only describe as happily disheveled: a plaid shirt and a loose fitting pair of khaki pants covered in daubs of paint. She had a pleasant, open face, almost childlike, crowned by a mass of beautifully unkempt brown hair. Her eyes pointed in slightly different directions, which had the unnerving effect of making it difficult to determine if she was actually looking at me.

She broke the silence by speaking first. "You must be new here. I'm Frances." I introduced myself and asked how long she had been in this space, which looked well used. "I got this in spring semester. The previous occupant cracked up, and I got to move from the Annex to here. I won't be in the studio lottery. How could I do better?"

I looked over at the painting, which was a mass of washes and loose brushstrokes, and asked, "Is that Gena Rowlands?"

"Yes!" Frances came over and hugged me. "You're the first person to recognize her."

It was difficult to make out a specific face from the riot of color, but the red lips and blonde hair were giveaways. The painting belonged in a much larger space. I asked, "How do you get a good look at it in this studio?"

"I open the door wide and lurk around the courtyard. I look like a sex pervert, but that's just an added benefit."

I said, "I don't recognize the film this comes from."

"That's because it's from television. *The Rifleman*."

"So the color choices are your own. That show was in black and white, wasn't it?" I asked.

Frances became animated. "When I imagine Gena's face, I always see her in color. She's a goddess."

"I bet you were crushed to find out *The Tarnished Angels* is in black and white."

She let out a whoop of delight. "Oh my god, you're right. But in my mind, Dorothy Malone is always in color, too."

"Well, at least we have *Written on the Wind*." I walked over to the table and picked up a drawing that resembled a scene from *Marnie*, but with a difference: Tippi Hedren, arms full of loot from the safe she has just robbed, bent over a desk getting her ass eaten by the boss's secretary—an improvement on the Hitchcock film.

Noticing which drawing I was looking at, she said, "Oh Tippi, she was so sexy but such a strange actress."

Wondering if her interest extended only to blondes, I asked, "Anna Magnani?"

"I'm weak in the knees thinking about her, darling." She elaborated, "Great actresses do what great painters do. They make a gazillion decisions per second and then figure out a way to project them, through the lens or through a frame, you know? It's so crazy, the amount of stuff that gets packed into every movement."

Her statement led to a discussion of how she chose a specific image from a film to adapt as a painting, and this in turn led to a long conversation about old movies in general, a topic that I, having worked at a video store in a gay neighborhood until a week before, knew about as well as anyone. We talked so intently that I didn't notice the sun disappearing, and with it, my last opportunity to catch a bus home. I admitted my lack of a vehicle and on campus housing, and Frances very kindly offered to let me stay with her until the first year students were able to move into their studios over the following weekend.

The next morning, I woke up on Frances's couch when her dog licked my face. I got myself together as best I could and the two of us had breakfast at the Saugus Café, reputed to be the last place James Dean ate before his fatal accident in Paso Robles. (Several other restaurants claimed this distinction, I later found out.) I mentioned that I wanted to pass by my apartment at some point, so I wouldn't have to wear the same clothes the whole week. Frances said, "I need to buy paint in town, if you don't mind the detour."

"Do you think I'll make it to my one o'clock critique class?" I asked seriously.

"You'll definitely show up before it's over," she said with the tone of someone who had done exactly that on many occasions.

A half hour later, we stopped by my apartment, and I checked my mail and packed a bag. After visits to a couple of art supply stores, we got back on the freeway. I asked Frances questions about how the school worked. She explained, "You'll want to stay on the good side of the faculty. If you don't have anything in common with someone, meet with them anyway and nod and smile. I've seen very good students ignore the faculty and get screwed when they give out scholarships."

"I had no idea."

She said, "It's worst for the smart ones. They understand very quickly that some instructors have nothing to say, so they ignore them. Terrible idea. Those faculty meetings are full of fragile egos. Never forget it if you want your financial aid to come through." She looked over at me and asked, "You *are* on financial aid, aren't you?" I nodded. "I've seen some performances. Trust fund babies pretending to be poor. Everyone falls for it until they come back from Christmas with a ski tan or start driving a BMW when the old Volvo breaks down one too many times."

"Oh, that's not me. I'm not carless and planning to live in my studio out of a sense of masochism."

Frances was on a roll: "There's a new way of thinking about art school that I don't understand at all. Some of my classmates use the word 'career' and I throw up in my mouth a little bit. I don't say it out loud, but I'm like, are you kidding me? Is this a corporation? What the hell is going on? I know it sounds so hippy dippy—and in a way equally pretentious—to say, no, this isn't a career, but I'm completely *ad nauseam* to even use that word. Is what we're doing right now a career move, or an act of self mutilation? Why do we do this? I don't think it's for a career."

I said, "The huge loans we take out have poisoned the system. Students are thrown into competition with each other. They're probably talking about the situation in the only way they know how."

She said, "Those loans are evil. A friend of mine skipped the country to avoid them. Now he can't come back. He's afraid if he does, the banks will find out and come after him. The only way to stop paying them for sure is to die. And we don't want that to happen." She gave me a quick glance and said, "We have to look out for whoever's real."

I said, "You know, someone said the same thing to me last week after registration."

"Oh yeah, who?"

"This guy named Paul. He drives a convertible and cruises the tearoom on I-5. Do you know him?"

"Paul?" Frances looked flabbergasted. "He graduated a few years ago. What was he doing on campus?"

I thought for a moment. "He was trying to get into the Annex. He said he had some things locked up in there."

"Watch out for that guy," she said as she touched my knee. "Have you heard the stories about him?"

"For example?" I asked.

"Students used to live in trailers in the parking lot, and everything was cool. But one day, Paul decided he'd take revenge on a ex-lover. He did a Lisa 'Left Eye' Lopes and set fire to his trailer." She got a crazy look on her face and said, "The house of love has burned to the ground."

"That's incredible."

"Somehow he never got punished, but since then, no more trailer living at Cal Arts."

"The 'good old days' I've heard so much about."

She said, "But wait, there's more. He came to class one day with his ass bleeding. A trucker had fucked him a little too hard. I have to say I admire his guts, but he's a piece of work." She paused. "I guess he's looking for a new generation to corrupt."

"If we aren't corrupted already."

We arrived at school at a quarter past two. I got to my class as it was adjourning for a break. I apologized to the instructor, explaining that I had no car and needed to do an urgent errand. I returned on time from the break and was careful to give the impression of a diligent student for the rest of the period.

I returned to Frances's studio after class, and we went to her place after a little shopping. We cooked dinner together, with her doing most of the work, as I was inept in the kitchen.

Over dinner, we talked about our pasts. She had gone to art school as an undergraduate in Kansas City. Her department was not very sympathetic. She said, "There was always a sense that if you called something queer or feminist or drew attention to the fact that you were a woman or whatever, even if it was specific to the painting, it was instantly assumed to be a limitation. It was like, yes, you are queer, but how are you going to make that bigger and more interesting to an actual audience?"

I asked, "Are these people still living in the '50s? Do we all have to be Pollock-style closet cases?"

"I know. It's crazy. Here the situation's totally different, but not always better. Some cerebral weirdos learn how to work the current political agenda that's being slung around. They can talk about queerness even if they're not queer. Believe me, I've gotten into trouble with some of the LUGS." I gave her a clueless look and she added, "Lesbians until graduation. The faculty and students all say, 'Ooh, that's great' whenever anyone declares herself in that way. There's a lot of support for art that's identity based, but of course, the work ends up having no sensuality, no bodily engagement at all. It's just illustrative. I want to say, 'Quit using that mouth to spout theory and eat my pussy!'" We both shrieked with laughter. Once we calmed down, she finished by saying, "These kids are all talk."

I said, "Hey, I feel like a cerebral weirdo sometimes, but I guess I'm not *all* talk. I'm here to find a way to make art."

"Aren't we all?" she asked.

"I considered myself primarily a writer until now." I looked into Frances's eyes. "Maybe I'm the enemy."

"Honey, if you're asking yourself that question, you're definitely *not* the enemy."

∞

The next morning, I went to the Art School office for the studio lottery. Fewer students than I expected showed up. Even an event as important as choosing a work space for the upcoming academic year couldn't get some people out of bed early. The man I had noticed on registration day was waiting for his turn. He was number one among the first year master's students, and he chose the last of the most desirable studios remaining, then left immediately afterward. I felt an urge to follow him, but I restrained myself. When my turn came, I chose a studio in the far corner of the Annex building. As a slip of paper with my name on it was pinned to a large chart on the office wall, I peered at the space chosen by the mystery man. It was adjacent but for a shaft of air to my studio, and was claimed by someone named Winston Smith.

∞

I arrived at the first meeting of my video class on time. The course was important because passing it gave access to the Art School's equipment: cameras, lights, and a simple editing system. As far as I could tell, everyone else was there for the same reason, but the instructor made an effort to turn Intro to Video into a real academic course. We watched a lot of video art.

As one of the longer works played, I looked around at my fellow students. Someone on the other side of the room interested me. He looked like a Latino version of Robert Smith from The Cure. His black hair had been teased up into the spiky shape of a fright wig. He was slightly chubby and wore black pants, a black suit jacket with a Bela Lugosi t-shirt under it, and conservative lace-up shoes. It was hard to tell in the dim bluish light emitted by the television monitor, but I thought I could detect some makeup on his face. His nails had been painted black. When the lights came up, I continued to look at the guy. He didn't seem to notice. When the instructor made a request that we pair up for the first assignment, I went directly over to him.

"What's your name?"

"Gregorio. I guess the teacher forgot to ask."

"Are you an MFA student?"

"No," he said with downcast eyes. "Fourth year BFA. I have a bachelor's from the University of New Mexico, but that wasn't good enough for them here. I'm a DIP."

"What's that?" I asked.

"Dissatisfied in placement. I have to schedule a review if I want an adjustment of my status." He was clearly annoyed to be talking about this.

The class went on break, and afterwards, Gregorio and I sat next to each other. The teaching assistant passed out photocopied instructions for the video cameras. When he came to Gregorio and me, he looked us up and down before handing over our copies. Once he was out of earshot, I whispered, "What attitude," and Gregorio laughed. I pointed and said, "Take a look at that." On the TA's bag slung across his empty chair was a Queer Nation sticker reading, "Dress for success. Wear a white penis."

"What the fuck?" Gregorio scowled, because, as far as either of us could tell, the TA was indeed dressed for success.

∞

After class, I asked Gregorio if he wanted to visit Frances in her studio. When we got there, she was blasting music again. I knocked loudly, but she didn't hear me until the song was over. Just as Gregorio was about to leave, she showed up at the door. We walked in, and I said, "Wow," when I saw her painting. It had changed drastically for the better. Somehow, the brushstrokes that looked chaotic before had begun to coalesce into a more recognizable likeness of Gena Rowlands. I couldn't figure out how she had done this, and I wanted to ask her about it, if such things were available for her to describe in words. I said, "Frances, this is Gregorio. He's new here, too."

He said, "Hi, I hope you don't mind if I look at your tapes."

"Of course not," she said. "They're a total mess, like everything else in this studio."

I said, "Except what counts, the painting on the wall."

"Thank you. I was about to take a break," she said as she opened a beer.

"It looks almost done."

She stepped back as far as she could and said, "You may be right. I don't want to overwork it. Maybe I should invite you to the studio on a regular basis to tell me when to quit painting." She looked at Gregorio, who was preoccupied with her cassettes, then looked at me and raised her eyebrows. I shrugged. She announced, "I feel like having a nice dinner. Want to come over, Gregorio?"

He nodded and asked, "How's your music collection at home?"

"That's where I keep all my records." At this, his face lit up.

I rode to her place in Gregorio's old Toyota truck. On the way, I said, "I hope I'm not keeping you from anything."

"No." He seemed a little uneasy. "I need to make friends anyway. And Frances seems fun. So do you." He might have wondered if this evening's dinner was a plot to seduce him. I wondered the same thing myself.

At Frances's, Gregorio went over to her records and started taking things off the shelves. I heard him mutter "American pressings" to himself with distaste. He saw a record cover with a large smudge of paint on it and shuddered. I decided to leave him alone and went to the kitchen. Soon after, we heard music coming from the living room: "Search and Destroy" from *Raw Power* by The Stooges. I looked in to see Gregorio lost in the music.

After a long dinner with lots of wine, we had to figure out the sleeping arrangements. There was no way Gregorio could drive back home. Frances and I agreed to share her bed, while our new friend would sleep on the couch. Upon hearing this, he had an expression I couldn't read; perhaps it was disappointment, or merely relief.

SEVEN

I didn't really think about my Friday class, Post Studio Art, while I was having dinner and getting drunk on Thursday night. I showed up a little late and very hung over. Around noon, I realized that I hadn't arranged moving into my new studio. I needed to call Moira, who had offered to help, and ask her if she could enlist Temo, because I didn't have his number. He was probably my only acquaintance with a credit card, and we needed to rent a truck, because I didn't want to make more than one trip for the move. I also had to pack up the contents of my apartment. I had very few possessions, but I was sure it would still be a major task. I was so busy with the first week of school that I forgot to get boxes. Feeling overwhelmed, I put my head in my hands. A while later, I noticed a couple of my classmates staring at me.

I learned from Frances that critiques in Post Studio Art ended only when the class ran out of things to say. This brought out the best and worst tendencies in students. On one hand, the course encouraged looking at artworks very carefully and discussing them in detail. Everyone had the luxury of hours to spend; there was nothing but time. On the other hand, during the long stretches that students were cooped up together, rivalries and petty vendettas flourished, all of them cloaked in the guise of critical discourse. There was also an unfortunate tendency to avoid talking about the actual artworks on display in favor of dissecting the verbiage around them. If a student misused a word or made an error in logic, the other students would pounce on it. On many occasions, the TA brought out a dictionary to adjudicate disputes. It reminded me of America's Miranda legal warning, "Anything you say can and will be used against you," though in this course, the right to remain silent was never exercised. In practice, everyone spoke, no matter how damaging this would be for their critiques.

The first half of the class ran so late that by the time the break came, the cafeteria was closed. Dinner consisted of whatever could be purchased from vending machines. This didn't seem to concern the instructor, Michael Asher, in the slightest. I was told the most anyone ever saw him eat was a cookie. He appeared to have no bodily functions at all, not even excusing himself to go to the toilet. He said very little, yet the class would continue whether he participated or not. He dozed off occasionally. Frances once saw him lying on the floor sleeping with his head propped up on the molding at the bottom of a cinder block wall. I thought being able to sleep under such circumstances was an impressive achievement in itself.

Asher's work as an artist consisted of "interventions" long before the word became fashionable. He convinced museums and other institutions to pay for rearranging their collections, sandblasting and rebuilding their walls, or producing rather unflattering publications based upon research in their archives. He was a punk, and elevated the prank to the level of an artistic statement. From what he said in class and the uproarious laughs he often emitted, it was obvious that he had a sense of humor. Somehow this escaped his most devoted students, who with deadening piety pursued "institutional critique"—a genre he inspired but a label he rejected. His disciples became inquisitors, dismantling the aesthetic aspects of an artwork, and in the process, flattening everything in their path. It was debased ideological criticism, with no way of distinguishing revelatory art from illustrative hackwork.

∞

The next day, Gregorio drove me to my apartment on his way to the record stores on Melrose. Before he dropped me off, I gave him a short tour of the neighborhood sights: Hyperion Avenue, where auto body shops alternated with sex clubs and gay bars; Bolzano's, where a ring of book thieves sold their acquisitions to the owner, a guy I'd had sex with (a fact I didn't reveal to Gregorio); Amok, where we stopped to look at records and books; Mondo Video A-Go-Go, the latest addition to Vermont Avenue's commercial strip, to the consternation of many, since it had the most tasteless window displays and stock imaginable at that time, a highlight being a whole section of videos about the junky coprophile punk GG Allin; House of Pies, the oldest diner in Los Feliz; the Hollyhock House designed by Frank Lloyd Wright, on top of a hill from which one could see the massive white Ennis House, another Wright building that threatened to slide off its foundation during the Northridge earthquake. I wasn't sure when I would see these places again, or if I'd live in the area after graduation. When I realized how many interesting things there were to show Gregorio, I regretted that I gave up my apartment. I had somehow convinced myself that the neighborhood was boring. Compared to remote suburbia, where I'd be spending the next two years, it was heaven on earth.

We went to buy boxes at a small printer in Los Feliz run by a Chinese couple. At the cash register, they kept a box of small ceramic ducks that no one ever bought. Above it was a sign reading, "Ducks do not quack," a sentence the proprietors didn't find as funny as I did. Afterwards, we went to the apartment. Gregorio said he could come by later if I needed anything. I said I didn't want to impose on him, and other friends of mine would be helping me move. All I needed to do was pack, a task better done alone. He looked a little let down. I grabbed him and kissed him on the lips, a gesture that made him uncomfortable. He stammered his goodbye and went to the door. After I saw him out, I spent a few minutes in the bathroom wiping lipstick off my face.

I cleared out my closet, which disgorged an appalling amount of clothing I no longer wore or even remembered owning. I drew up a list of things I would need in the studio. I filled out a forwarding order and took a break by walking to the post office to drop it off. I made a few last calls from my telephone. I relished the convenience, since at school, I'd have to rely on pay phones. I began to wonder if I made the right decision. When thinking about a lackluster first week of classes, I felt some apprehension.

As happy as I was for the help, I dreaded the arrival of Moira and Temo. I had the vague impression that I was trapped in a French farce. I couldn't talk to Temo in a way that implied we were friends. As far as Moira knew, all our conversations had taken place in her presence, and we basically couldn't stand each other. I assumed that Moira hadn't a clue about Temo's sex life, something I barely understood myself. I wondered what cover stories he told his conservative, overprotective family. I doubted they were even aware that he worked at a radical bookstore. I sometimes fantasized about being a fly on the wall in his therapist's office, but then I realized that a guy as arrogant and spoiled as he was probably wouldn't see the need for therapy. A Spanish word my friend Raúl had taught me years before popped into my head: *fresa*. Literally, it meant strawberry, but in Mexico City slang, it referred to preppy rich kids whose delicate beauty, sweet smell, and juicy taste required great care to cultivate.

My friends arrived right on time, and we prepared the move without a problem. It involved Moira driving her car separately to my apartment and taking the stuff I couldn't bring to my new studio, including records and a thrift store stereo, some cookware, and a box of books I was confident I'd be able to find in the school library. She drove this load to her apartment and waited for us to pick her up before we got on the freeway to Santa Clarita.

I had a period alone with Temo, and I wondered if he would want to get fucked in my empty apartment. He dropped no hints that this was the case. I went a little crazy, knowing that this would be our last chance to see each other for a long time. I wondered what was going through his head, and I came to the conclusion that he wanted to avoid an emotional scene. I might have been giving him too much credit; maybe he had no emotions to avoid.

When our work was finished, I grabbed his ass. He swatted my hand away. I wouldn't take no for an answer. I unbuttoned his pants, pulled them down, and started to rub his hole. I could tell he hadn't douched. I bent him over the kitchen table and slid my hard cock into him, with no lube and no condom. He whined and groaned. I pounded his ass without saying a word, and arrived at the point of ejaculating inside him. He reached back and grabbed my ass so that I couldn't pull out, and closed his hole around my cock. It was as though he had a second mouth down there and was sucking me off. He ejaculated and left a long splatter down the leg of the table and on the floor beneath it. For the first time in our interactions—I wouldn't call it a relationship—he gave me his opinion about the sex: "That was fantastic." He grabbed a roll of paper towels and started wiping himself off. He smelled like a gutter after a rain. We both went to the bathroom. I took a shower while he sat on the toilet, then he joined me and I washed his body. As we rinsed off, we looked into each other's eyes. It was an uncharacteristically tender moment, one that made me suspect that this would be the last time we'd ever have sex.

We dried ourselves with paper towels, because the linens had already been packed. I found a stray plastic bag and placed the mess in it to throw away. I watched Temo get dressed in the afternoon light streaming through my window. At that moment he looked absolutely ravishing: from the front he was an impeccable *macho*, the summit of Mexican manhood; from the back, he was a fucked-out slut with an ass itching to be destroyed. He took a moment to admire himself in the full-length mirror on the wall of my bedroom. He broke the mood by turning to me and saying, "Stop staring at me. And don't do it around Moira, okay? She knows nothing."

"No problem. Let's hit the road."

∞

Once at Cal Arts, surrounded by students moving into their studios, I understood that no matter how much we tried to appear normal, the three of us were the oddest trio in a place reputed to be a haven for weirdos. Our conversations were strained enough that we could have been mistaken for family members, if it weren't so obvious from the way we looked that we couldn't be blood relatives. Temo and Moira spoke Spanish to each other, and I spoke English to them, unless I was saying something simple like a curse word or *¡Ven acá!* (come here).

Gregorio was moving into the studio across the hall from me, so we saw each other constantly while we were working. Temo gave him the contemptuous look he gave all Chicanos—ironic for a professed leftist, but undoubtedly the result of a deeply ingrained prejudice. For his part, Gregorio looked like he might kill Temo, something I found amusing. I flattered myself by thinking that their rivalry had something to do with me. The only time they talked to each other was when Temo briefly left a box blocking the hallway. Gregorio shouted, "*Güero*, you gotta move your shit!"

Temo shot back, "*Coño*." He moved the box into my studio, and as he did, said the word *maricón* under his breath. I was thankful that Gregorio seemed not to have heard this.

At one point when we were almost finished, Moira went off to use the bathroom and left Temo and me in the studio. We were sweaty and hot, and I got a whiff of him. He smelled like sex. I kissed him passionately. He let me do it and obviously enjoyed himself. When we were done, he handed me a slip of paper with his email address: bolsillodepayaso@aol.com. "Use it any time you want."

"I've never had email, but I guess I'll get an account through the school."

"Welcome to the '90s, *flaco*," he said in a tone so condescending it made me wonder why I had kissed him.

"What does *bolsillo de payaso* mean?"

He whispered, "Clown's pocket. It's slang for an asshole so stretched out that anything can fit inside."

I smiled broadly and said, "Thanks," just as Moira returned. When I looked in her direction, I noticed Gregorio's studio door wide open. He must have seen me kissing Temo. I said to Moira, "Thank you, too. I couldn't have done it without you." As I said it, I heard Gregorio's door slam.

Moira said, "It wasn't too difficult. I promise I'll take good care of your stereo."

"Do you two want to get a bite to eat?" I asked.

Temo looked at his watch and said, "No, I'm supposed to have dinner with my parents in a while."

I waved goodbye as they drove away, leaving me alone in my new situation. I went back and started arranging things in the studio.

E I GHT

The next week passed uneventfully, except for my interactions with men on campus. On Tuesday, I saw Winston Smith again. The week before, I had come to the second half of my critique class, and he had only attended the first half, so I didn't know he was enrolled in it. His hair was a different color, red this time, though it wasn't very bright, because he hadn't bleached his hair before dyeing it. I tried to figure out what he was like as a person, but he frustrated my efforts by not saying a single word over the course of three hours.

In Intro to Video I saw Gregorio, who pointedly took a seat across the room from me when he arrived. I regretted not closing my studio door before I kissed Temo over the weekend, but there was nothing I could do to change that, so I took it upon myself to move next to him. I quietly said, "That guy means nothing to me."

Gregorio gave me a sidelong glance. "It looked like you're in love with him."

"It was a goodbye kiss. I may never see him again."

"Huh." Gregorio was unconvinced.

"The woman I was with is one of my oldest friends. She tried to date him, poor dear, but he's totally gay, and as soon as she's not looking, he gets very… friendly." This story met with a skeptical look. "I guess things got a little out of hand. We should have shut the door. I'm sorry."

"Sounds like your friend is the one you should apologize to."

"I'll leave that to Cuauhtémoc."

Gregorio laughed. "What a pretentious name."

∞

I spent a lot of time in Frances's studio during fall semester. My own was barren and reminded me that I wasn't making art, so I avoided it. Frances never seemed to attend class, and I asked her about this. She said, "Independent studies are the best. I get to paint every day and talk about my work with the people I choose. This place is so hostile to painting that I have to make my own curriculum."

"Still? Cal Arts was all about conceptual art at the beginning, but that was a long time ago."

"It's like Catholic guilt, no matter how hard you try, it never goes away. And here the original sin is painting."

"Never mind that some of their most successful alumni have been painters," I said.

"It was different in the '70s, not so well defined. Now everything's become academic, and I don't mean that in a good way." She plunged her brush into a jar of brownish walnut oil, then took off her rubber gloves and sat down next to me. "Are you and Gregorio getting along?" she asked with a tone of concern in her voice.

"Yeah, why?"

She said, "Be good to him. He's sensitive, and he's having a hard time here."

"Let's go visit him." The two of us walked the short distance to his studio. There was a muffled noise inside. "Maybe we should go to my studio instead." As I said this, Gregorio opened the door. He wasn't alone.

Somewhat startled, Frances said, "Hello, Paul. You work quick."

Paul smoothed his hair and said, "If I'd known you were coming, I'd have baked a cake." In the harsh light, he could have been mistaken for a patient at a fancy asylum.

There was a palpable tension between Paul and Frances, who turned to me and said, "Someone keeps coming back for more."

He shot back, "Oh, pshaw, I don't mean any harm. Just spreading the good news."

Gregorio broke the uncomfortable silence when he produced a VHS tape from a shopping bag and handed to it Frances. "Here, I think you'll like this."

"*The Neon Bible*." Frances was overjoyed at the prospect of seeing a Gena Rowlands vehicle that she hadn't used for a painting yet. She hugged him and asked, "How did you find it?"

"I have my ways," Gregorio said, smiling.

Paul made his excuses and left, and Frances followed him out, leaving me alone in the studio with Gregorio. I asked if he'd bought any new records. With great enthusiasm, he showed me a copy of Pere Ubu's *The Modern Dance*, the original pressing, never properly released in the US. The cover reproduced a line drawing of a dancer from a Chinese proletarian ballet against an industrial background that was a stylized version of Cleveland, the city where the band was founded. He put the record on the turntable, and we sat down on midcentury modern chairs that Gregorio had bought at a thrift store out in the desert. He was a remarkably skilled shopper, never paying much for beautiful things, except when it came to records. That was where all his money went. He had slowly built a small but remarkable collection, arranged on a single shelf in chronological order. When music came up in conversation in his presence, which was frequently, and the subject was a specific album, I would notice him talking under his breath. Once Frances mentioned

Joy Division's *Unknown Pleasures*, and I heard him whispering, "June 15, 1979," its release date. He was the album savant.

When the side of the record ended, I said, "You've never told me where you come from in New Mexico."

He asked, "Are you sure you want to know?" I nodded. "Truth or Consequences."

"Wow, that couldn't have been easy. Were you the only kid there with your taste in music?"

"The only brown one. My dad is the town therapist, but he isn't very good. Too judgmental." It occurred to me that he might have meant to say his dad wasn't a very good father. "When I was fourteen, I saw Derek Jarman's video for 'The Queen Is Dead' on MTV, and my life was never the same again. As soon as I could, I went to the record stores in Las Cruces and El Paso and bought everything by The Smiths. When I moved to Albuquerque, my habit got really serious. I learned that US pressings of records sound like shit compared to UK and European ones. Vinyl, I mean. CDs are for yuppie scum. I decided to buy only the best copies of albums from the time when rock music was great. I worked backwards from 1986 to 1972."

"I'd love to hear your collection."

"Any time. I'm used to listening to records alone, but it's a little sad," he said.

"Hanging out and listening to music is what I thought art school would be about."

He put on the first side of David Bowie's *"Heroes"* and we sat back and listened in silence for a while. "Joe the Lion" came on, and I sang along to the line, "Nail me to my car and I'll tell you who you are." When it was over, I said, "I used to think that song was about getting fucked in a car. Then I found out it was about Chris Burden, who actually did get nailed to his Volkswagen for art."

He turned down the volume and said, "One night, my dad caught me fooling around with a guy in the back of a car. He was really angry. You'd think a therapist would be more understanding, but not him. Now I don't tell my parents anything about my sex life. The less they know, the better."

"Are you the only son?"

"Yeah. I have a sister." He looked down. "She's at Yale now."

"The School of Art?"

"Hell, no. Law school. I'm the family fuck up."

I said, "Join the club."

There was a knock at the door. Frances came in and asked, "May I join your little party?"

Gregorio said, "Sure. Any requests?"

"*This Nation's Saving Grace.*"

"Sorry, I don't have any later Fall records."

Perplexed, she asked, "Do you hate Brix Smith?"

"No. It's just that after a certain point, the albums started sounding more produced. I liked them when they recorded live in the studio, and the album covers looked like phone doodles." Gregorio had a very serious expression on his face.

I said, "Your heart is easily broken, isn't it?"

"Um, yeah." He looked at his shoes. They were beautifully shined, as they would have to be, I thought, since he sees so much of them.

Frances asked, "Are you doing costumes for Halloween?"

I grabbed Gregorio by the waist and said, "Vivienne Westwood and Malcolm McLaren."

"Who's Vivienne and who's Malcolm?"

I smiled. "We're still working that out."

Gregorio pried himself away from me. "No plans yet."

I said, "I can't do anything that involves makeup, because I have to be in class the next morning, and who knows if I'll be able to wash properly before then?" The opportunities for attending to personal hygiene were few and far between in the studios. "Maybe I'll be a ghost. If only I had a white sheet."

"You're no fun." Frances was hoping we'd be up for a wild time. "I may go as Lady Godiva."

Gregorio took out a copy of *Hex Enduction Hour,* and put on the song "Hip Priest." He said, "Maybe I'll be a priest," and rubbed his hands together. Eight minutes later, the song was over, and Frances invited us to her place for dinner. I decided to behave sensibly and not stay out too late. I slept in my studio after Gregorio, who didn't have a single drink, dropped me off at school.

∞

The night of the Halloween party, I arrived dressed as a ghost, with eye-holes cut out and the word "Boo!" scrawled in marker being my only concessions to craft in the making of a costume. Gregorio was wearing a priest's collar and cassock. Frances had somehow gotten hold of a nun's habit for the occasion. I saw Paul dressed as a pirate stalking the halls.

The Main Gallery, such a big space that only registration and a massive party could fill it up, was as alive as I had ever seen it. The music was wretched and served the sole purpose of drowning out any conversation. The floor of the place seethed with bodies attempting the preliminaries of sexual congress, fueled by a punch that tasted like kerosene mixed with a children's fruit drink.

Winston was nowhere to be seen at the party. Disappointed, I drank a bit more than I should have. I went around looking for anyone I knew. I encountered Paul first, and he took me to Gregorio, who was alone. (Frances had found a lady friend to hook up with.) He proposed that Paul and I come back to his studio for some absinthe, which I had never tried. We left and started walking to the Annex. In the corner of a landing, we discovered Winston, naked and motionless.

I checked to make sure he was still breathing and found that he was only very drunk. In the dim light of the stairwell, I scrutinized Winston's body as carefully as I could without appearing to stare. He had the hairiest legs I had ever seen, and a very large penis with a foreskin that covered the whole head. He also had some chest hair, but his belly was hairier.

Gregorio asked me, "Do you know that guy?"

"Not exactly, but I know where his studio is. He's got a key in his hand. Let's take him there." There was no sign of his clothes.

The three of us picked Winston up, and he barely stirred. I took his shoulders, Gregorio took his legs, and Paul took the middle, expressing delight that there was a penis in front of his face. We carefully descended the stairs and walked down the long hallway toward the exit. I led the way to his studio, and Paul tried the key, which worked. We deposited Winston on his futon, and Gregorio and I collapsed on the available chairs in the dark. The only illumination came from courtyard lights through the wide open door. Paul hovered over Winston's naked body. I dozed off briefly.

I awoke to a slurping sound. I looked at Gregorio. He was staring at Paul, whose head was bobbing up and down, sucking the hard cock of the unconscious Winston. We spectators were frozen in place, not knowing what to do. There was a grunt, almost inaudible, an indication that Winston was coming. Soon afterward, Paul stopped. He cleared his throat, stood up, adjusted his pants, and stumbled out of the studio. I went over to Winston, who was lying on his back, and turned him on his side to ensure he wouldn't choke if he vomited. I asked Gregorio what he wanted to do, and he said he was too drunk to drive home. I invited him to spend the night with me. We fell asleep on my futon in our costumes.

NINE

After our Tuesday critique class, Winston approached and said, "Thank you for helping me at the party." These were the first words he ever spoke to me, and I was surprised by his accent. It sounded Slavic or Greek, but not exactly either, mixed with German.

I was tempted to ask him right away where he was from, but instead I said, "You were naked and passed out in the stairwell. Did you find your clothes?"

"No. There is something else." We walked together down one of the school's many blank hallways, and he said in a low voice, "I have a problem. A drip coming from my penis."

"Hmm, did you have sex at the Halloween party?"

"I am not sure. I was extremely drunk." He had a look of anxiety on his face.

"I was too, but I think I know what happened. Three of us carried you back to your studio, and one was a very naughty boy. Do you mind if I do a little investigating? I'll have to tell one other person." He shrugged. We walked directly to Gregorio's studio. I introduced him to Winston, and I explained that Paul could have infected both of them. I asked, "Did Paul suck you off?"

Gregorio looked embarrassed and said, "Yeah, last week. But I don't have any symptoms."

"I'm going to talk to Paul, unless one of you wants to." They both shook their heads. I went to Frances's studio to get his phone number, then I called him from the nearest pay phone.

I said, "I want to speak to you about Halloween."

"Oh, whyever would you want to do that?" he asked with an air of indifference.

"Cut the shit, Paul. You gave someone the clap, and we need your help."

"I don't see how that's possible," he protested. "I don't have any symptoms, dearie."

"They don't always show, Typhoid Mary. I've got two friends here whose cocks you sucked, and one of them is dripping. We need to go to the Gay and Lesbian Center, preferably tomorrow." There was dead silence on the line. "Come on, it's the least you can do," I insisted. "Testing and treatments are free. All we need is a ride. And for you to get treated, too."

"I'd rather not."

"Hey, now that I have your number, I can give it to the boys you infected, and to the Los Angeles County Health Department."

"Oh lord, if you insist," he sighed. "What time tomorrow?"

"No later than ten thirty. Testing begins at eleven. Meet us in the Annex, okay?"

"Yes, Nurse Ratched," he whined. "You're no fun anymore."

"I'll be fun again once we take care of this little problem."

He said, "See you tomorrow," and hung up.

I walked back to the studios and found Gregorio and Winston enjoying themselves. The soundtrack to *The Great Rock'n'Roll Swindle* was playing at top volume. Between tracks, I told them that everything was arranged, and that we'd get a ride the next morning.

There was a smear of lipstick on Winston's face that could only have come from Gregorio. Once I noticed it, I couldn't look at anything else. Winston said, "I have a meeting with an instructor tomorrow morning."

I said, "Write a note saying you have to postpone due to a doctor's appointment. Anyone would understand. We need to get there early. It's first come, first served."

They both looked at me and said, "Thank you."

∞

The next day, Paul was as good as his word and arrived at the Annex reasonably on time. He drove us to Hollywood, and we checked in at the desk of the Gay and Lesbian Center a few minutes after they opened for testing. We went through the bureaucratic steps, passing in and out of small offices, getting blood drawn, giving urine samples, sticking swabs up our asses, and talking to counselors. I got done with the tests first and waited in the lobby. One by one, my companions limped over to me. I invited them to sit, but they preferred to stand. The treatment for gonorrhea was two painful shots, one in each ass cheek.

I thought it would be best to take a walking tour of Hollywood lasting until the soreness went away. We saw the sights, such as they were, on the Walk of Fame and found a cheap restaurant where we could stand at the counter. I told them about the former hustler strip along Selma Avenue, half a block south of the Center, near the YMCA. Having just left a clap clinic, they were less than excited to hear about the exploits of decades past. The counselors told them to refrain from sexual activity for two weeks, by which time we would have our test results.

Gregorio asked if we could go to Aron's Records, and Paul insisted on driving us there. We stayed at the store until just before Parking Enforcement started towing along Highland Avenue at three p. m. As we got in the car, Paul said, "I have a little errand I need to run."

Paul had a sensible aversion to making left turns in traffic, so he maneuvered his way around the block and headed south on Vine. At Beverly Boulevard, he turned right and then right again at Orange Avenue. He parked outside a two story Spanish style building and told us to wait in the car. After a while, he returned and told us we could come in with him. He explained, "We're going to pay a call on an old friend from our alma mater. When I was a sprightly young thing, John Boskovich was frightening people as a graduate student. At the same time, the poor dear, who was prisoner to parental expectations, attended USC Law School. To this day, John's the only person I've ever known who simultaneously received an MFA and a law degree at two different schools. She has her moods, but there's a brilliant mind in there… somewhere."

As we climbed the steps to his apartment, I noticed more than one surveillance camera pointed in our direction. A stocky, balding guy opened the door and scrutinized us briefly. He said, "Okay," and let us inside. Paul made the introductions. We all shook his hand, but it was hard to look him in the eye because his apartment distracted us.

I said, "Your place is incredible."

"Thanks," he said with a slightly bored air. "Welcome to the Psycho Salon. It's an environment I've been creating over the last couple of years. Have a look around, but please don't touch anything. The cleaning lady came today."

I had never seen anything like the interior. Curtains in bright pink velvet against acid green walls created a contrast that almost vibrated. We stepped onto a large round black carpet with a pink pentagram on it. There was plenty of furniture upholstered in naugahyde of various colors, and in one case, camouflage. In front of the large windows were statues of Hindu deities converted into lamps on pedestals that bore inscriptions. I asked, "Are those quotations from T. S. Eliot?"

"The *Four Quartets*. Let me show you the rest of the apartment." We passed into a room painted lavender and yellow. Almost every square inch of wall space was covered with art, framed Polaroid photographs arranged in series and separated by thick mats. I asked him if I could stay there and take a close look at them, and he said, "Of course. I have to talk to Paul about, um, something." The group dispersed.

The Polaroids themselves were fairly nondescript, and most were out of focus, though it wasn't clear to me at first whether the fuzziness was due to intention or the limitations of the medium. I concluded the former once I got a close look at the titles that had been printed on the images and mats, including "Portrait of the artist and dead boyfriend, September 9, 1996," a date less than two months before; "Last photo of dead boyfriend"; "Pig Bottom"; "Frances Farmer's Revenge"; and my favorite, "Semiotics of Trade: You should have stayed with that old fairy in Redondo Beach." There were names I didn't recognize—Raymond Lee, Mike Murphy, David Rimanelli, Chris Wilder—friends, I supposed; still among the living, I hoped. John returned to the room with a small paper bag in his hand. I said, "My condolences."

He responded blankly, "I surround myself with people who care about me." It was difficult to discern whether this was a sincere utterance or a quotation like so many others around the apartment. To change the subject, which was surely painful, he said, "Since you're such an avid reader, take a look at this." He led me to the laundry room, where the walls were covered with reviews of his film *Without You, I'm Nothing*, a collaboration with Sandra Bernhard. The two were no longer friends, or so I gathered from the expression on his face.

Oblivious, I asked the wrong question, "Have you made any films since this one?"

John's face fell for a second, then he recovered and said with a manic edge, "I've got lots of scripts in the works. A Kerouac adaptation I did on spec a few years ago with Meg Cranston is attracting some heat these days." He seemed to go blank again, and he wandered out of the room. I was left alone with his severe black washer-dryer set. I went to the kitchen. Although I was told not to touch anything, I saw no harm in opening a drawer. Inside I found not only utensils but quotations from Sylvia Plath poems. I opened another drawer, then cabinets, and every time I was confronted with texts. Even the trash can had an inscription: "Boskovich Farms, Incorporated. Family Pride Since 1915." John was the son of a grower with large land holdings in Oxnard. I wondered what his family thought about his art; I needed no explanation of what he thought about them.

I had to piss, and I found a bathroom with the door ajar at the end of a narrow room with walls, desk, and doors covered entirely in silver leaf. I moved a clear plastic chair aside so I could pass through. The bathroom gave an indication of what the rest of the apartment looked like before it had been so aggressively redecorated. The walls were covered with ceramic tiles characteristic of Los Angeles buildings from the 1920s and '30s, in this instance, bright yellow with black trim.

On impulse, I decided to leave the bathroom by way of a different door than the one through which I entered. If I had given it a moment's thought, I would have realized that the door gave onto John's bedroom. I went in, and all around I saw shiny things hanging on walls painted vivid violet. There were also several closed circuit television monitors, which must have been connected to the cameras I saw earlier, and others besides. The busy, paranoiac décor kept me from registering immediately what was happening on the bed: Winston sucking off John, whom I had seen only a short time before. Both parties were fully clothed. From what I could tell during the brief moment I saw them, they were having a good time.

I quickly went back to the living room, where I saw Paul and Gregorio reclining on a large circular divan covered with throw pillows. The scene looked completely different from what I saw upon entering, and I couldn't figure out how I had become disoriented. Perhaps this was the main intent of the apartment's design, like a casino that encouraged visitors to lose track of time in a cool, darkened space full of sensory stimuli. Gregorio looked up and asked, "Where's Winston?"

I said, "I think he'll be joining us shortly."

Paul looked at his watch and said, "Now that I've made my delivery, I can go. That is, unless you boys are up for another diversion while we wait out rush hour traffic."

Gregorio shook his head and was about to say something when Winston appeared at the doorway looking a bit rumpled. Then John emerged, adjusting his crotch. He said, "I have to throw you out. I'm going to see *Love Is Colder Than Death* at the New Beverly."

Paul said, "Thank you for the pleasant interlude."

"Yes, see you later," Winston said, as though he had plans to meet John again.

As we left, Gregorio asked a question to which he didn't really want to know the answer, directed at both of us, "What were you doing all that time?"

"Examining the flatware," I said.

"John showed me the CCTV system," Winston said. "He can watch what happens around the building, and he writes a list of everything he sees."

Gregorio said, "Weird."

On the drive to Santa Clarita, Paul looked over at me in the front seat and said, "We've just visited the lair of a haunted soul. He hasn't entertained in the last couple of months, but I convinced him to make an exception for us." Thinking about this, we passed the greater part of the hour long trip in silence.

Once we arrived on campus, Paul disappeared, probably to find an old trick or someone to whom he could sell drugs. Gregorio went home. When we were alone, I scolded Winston, "You're not supposed to have sex for two weeks after your shots."

He replied, "If I want to suck a Serbian cock, what does it matter?" I thought about the Polaroid with the words "Pig Bottom" on it and laughed to myself. I turned to go to my studio, and he caught me by the arm, looked me in the eye and said, "Thank you for showing me Hollywood. It was wonderful."

∞

The next day I woke up and realized that I had missed the election of 1996. Bill Clinton was reelected, while the House and Senate remained in Republican control, something that would not bode well for the President. All of this had happened without my vote. Along with most of my fellow students, I was living in an alternate reality sheltered from the outside world. We talked about what we took to be politics, but we had no direct involvement in the political process. Winston, as a foreigner, could not vote, but I had no excuse for myself, and I felt like a fool.

I went to see Winston and found him working. He turned his easel around to show me his painting. I was amazed to see a portrait of Enver Hoxha. It bore the marks of many revisions. In places the impasto had become quite thick. He had started with a thin coat of underpainting, still visible near the edges, and a buildup of paint protruded near the center. The portrait showed only Hoxha's face and a bit of his shoulders, and was roughly life size. It reminded me of the artwork appearing in the 1940s adaptation of *The Picture of Dorian Gray*, a grotesque color surprise at the climax of a black and white movie. I told Winston this, and he looked pleased. The paint showed few brushstrokes, as a lot of it had been applied with a knife. The palette was almost fluorescent, with regions of complementary colors in close juxtaposition, a technique used in professional illustrations for greater impact. The painting was far too strange and obsessive to be taken for an illustrator's work. I asked, "Have you shown this to many people?"

"All were silent. Why does no one talk to me?"

"You're a painter in a school that doesn't embrace painting, so perhaps people don't feel confident talking about what you do," I said, frowning. "And I don't think anyone knows who Hoxha is."

He looked surprised. "You recognize him?"

"I do. Long story." I looked at him. "Are you Albanian?"

"Yes."

"That's why I couldn't place your accent." I asked, "How did you get the name Winston?"

He said, "Also a long story."

I noticed the time and said, "I think I should go to class," with a gloomy tone.

"To hear a profound discussion of a cardboard box?" We both laughed at that.

I asked, "Have you met Frances?" He seemed to nod, then corrected himself and shook his head. I said, "Let's go find her." We went over to her studio, and I introduced the two painters. Soon they were engaged in a heated conversation. I excused myself to go to a class where, as predicted, a serious debate about a piece of hastily made and ill-conceived sculpture was in progress. Once I had my fill of this, I left. Upon my return, I saw that Winston and Frances were still talking, and they had been joined by Gregorio, who was poring over Frances's music collection as usual.

At dinner that evening, there was less wine to go around, and we got only a little tipsy. The conversation was lively. At some point, Winston turned on Frances's television, and seeing that she had cable, he became transfixed. With every commercial break, he would change the channel and watch another program. We had to drag him away at the end of the evening. Gregorio was sober enough to drive us back to campus, and we all squeezed into his truck.

Winston said, "On American television I see nothing but animals and World War II battles. Who killed Bambi? It was the Nazis!"

∞

Two weeks after our first appointments, Winston, Gregorio, and I (but not Paul) went back to the Center for results. Mine were all negative. Because Winston and Gregorio had been exposed to gonorrhea and been treated, they had more blood drawn. They were told that they wouldn't be notified of the results of those tests unless they came out positive. Each of us heard an announcement from his respective counselor: a new class of AIDS drugs had been approved and was now in use to treat patients. Antiretroviral therapy involving a combination of medicines prevented HIV infections from becoming full-blown AIDS for a very long time, and in many cases, reduced the viral load of patients to such low levels that antibodies could no longer be detected in the blood. If the patient complied well with treatment by taking the medications every day, then AIDS, which up to that point was almost always fatal, would become a manageable chronic illness, like diabetes. Patients who were once considered unlikely to survive more than a few months began to think of their lives as decades longer. The catch, as with so many things made possible by modern medicine, was the expense. A cocktail of antiretroviral drugs, which had to be changed periodically to prevent resistance, cost roughly the same as art school tuition or regular psychoanalysis, which is to say, it was a luxury. Except that it wasn't. We were being told, pay lots of money and live; be poor and die. Welcome to America. The counselor ended by stressing that HIV was still very serious, and this development should not be interpreted as a license to have unsafe sex, although a significant number of gay men must have interpreted it exactly that way.

After getting our test results, we walked to the Max Factor Museum on Highland, which impressed Gregorio, the only one of us who wore makeup. Then we went to Aron's Records, which was a long walk away. The boulevards in Los Angeles were much farther apart than my friends had expected. Winston said, "This is a city built for giants, like my old neighborhood. Karl-Marx-Allee is so wide that you must run across the street when the light changes."

I said, "You lived in Berlin."

"Yes, for a few years. I went to university there."

We took a bus back to Hollywood Boulevard, and Gregorio searched for his truck. He remembered it was parked near the First Baptist Church, where hustlers used to lounge on the front steps in the 1970s. On the way back to Santa Clarita, we discussed our test results, and that led to a conversation about our sexual histories.

"Before I came to Cal Arts I had a relationship with a guy who liked to be fisted," I said.

Winston laughed. "A lot of this in Berlin. *Faust ficken!*" He sighed. "I am lucky I am not HIV positive." He declined to provide more details, and I didn't press him.

"Well, fisting is safe, if it's done well," I offered.

"But how do you get off?" Gregorio asked.

"Oh, blowjobs from satisfied partners." Gregorio didn't say anything about his own experiences, so I asked, "What about our Halloween priest?"

"It's complicated." He paused. "I went through puberty very early, and I was that evil twelve year old, sucking and getting sucked. A whole bunch of us would have sex together. It was great. Anyway, my dad knew something was up, and he freaked out. He punished me and lectured me. It was humiliating. Since then, I've been sort of shy." Winston put his hand on Gregorio's knee, and we rode for a while in silence.

I asked Gregorio, "What did you buy at Aron's?"

"I found an import copy of Wire's *154*." When I mentioned *Pink Flag*, he smiled and said, "You think I'm an amateur? That must have been the second or third album I bought when I started collecting. It's essential."

I asked Winston, "What do you listen to?"

"Punk. This is obvious. But other things, too, like opera."

I said, "I haven't listened much to contemporary music since Kurt Cobain died."

"That is *not* punk," Winston said firmly.

"I don't buy anything released after *The Queen Is Dead*," Gregorio said. "The Smiths changed my life. I don't know if I'll ever forgive them for breaking up so soon."

I asked, "You never got into Morrissey's solo career?"

"No one could be as perfect as Johnny Marr. Without him, the music is just a pale imitation. The melodies and guitar playing on those Smiths records are the real thing." He looked as though he was going to cry, so I refrained from asking about *Your Arsenal*, a great Morrissey solo record produced by Mick Ronson, the guitarist who invented the sound of the Spiders from Mars. I brought up *Transformer* by Lou Reed, and this inspired a detailed comparison of the musical contributions of co-producers Ronson and David Bowie. I asked Gregorio if he ever wanted to collect albums by The Velvet Underground, and a look of panic came over him. He said, "I can't even start. So many bootlegs."

I said, "An obsessive. I love it."

TEN

Gregorio had been busy for a few weeks preparing a body of work to show in the review that would determine whether he advanced to the MFA program. I visited his studio to see what he had done. On top of wooden pedestals, he had constructed small sculptures that looked like the models a designer would make for a theatrical production. They consisted of panels of stiff paper painted with gouache in abstract patterns, mostly in pale colors. He lit them from above for dramatic effect. Winston and Frances also came by to admire them.

The next day, he had his review and officially became an MFA student, starting in the spring term. He'd be only one semester behind his classmates, and perhaps there'd be a way of making that up later. He came to see me with Winston and said, "Now let's celebrate." He told us to meet him at his studio at four.

Gregorio drove us to the house he shared with a couple of Film School students in Saugus. The timing was perfect, because they were in class until seven, and we would have the place to ourselves. We pulled into the driveway of a standard suburban house painted an inoffensive shade of tan, one of the few colors approved by the homeowners' association.

When we got inside, I immediately noticed a swimming pool in the back yard. I asked, "Is the pool clean?"

"Yeah, but not heated." Before Gregorio finished saying that, Winston was already stripping off his clothes. I followed his lead, and in a minute we were both naked.

"C'mon, let's have a swim," I said, taking Gregorio by the hand. At the edge of the pool, he carefully laid out his clothes in a pile. Winston and I jumped in and screamed, because the water was very cold. Gregorio stepped in and discovered the same thing. We braved the pool for only a little while until we had to get out. Dripping with chlorinated water and shivering, I asked, "Where's the shower?"

Gregorio quickly brought towels and turned on the faucet for us. As we waited for the water to warm up, I felt myself getting an erection, something the frigid water in the pool had prevented. Winston got in, and I took Gregorio's hand again as I entered the shower. Once the three of us were naked and in close quarters, we started to play around, just jerking each other's cocks. We soaped up and scrubbed each other's backs and caressed each other.

Without talking, we all dried off and made our way to Gregorio's bed, which was huge, a size called "California king." Gregorio pulled me partly off the bed so that my head dangled over the edge. He put his hard cock in my mouth and it slid down my throat. His cock was dark brown, circumcised, and not very large. I had no trouble swallowing it. Winston started sucking my hard cock, and when he took breaks, he rose to kiss Gregorio. Winston got on top of me and teased my cock with his asshole, with no penetration. I pulled Gregorio's cock from my mouth and sat up. I got behind Winston and started eating his ass. Winston turned Gregorio around and ate his ass. We were all in a line on the bed. I was getting lost in all the hair around Winston's hole, but I found it well enough to spit on it. I mounted him from behind and inserted my cock without a condom. He gave no complaint. His hole was tight at first but relaxed quickly. Gregorio rolled over and saw me pumping away. He guided Winston's face toward his cock so he could have it sucked. Winston was the "lucky Pierre" in our trio, getting fucked and sucking at the same time. Gregorio came quickly, but I didn't see any semen, because Winston swallowed every drop. I wondered if he wanted me to come in his ass. My guess was that he did, but instead I came all over the patch of black hair on the small of his back. He turned to look at me as if to ask, "Why did you pull out?" He rolled onto his back and started to masturbate. Gregorio and I saw the injustice of anatomy: this man who from all appearances was a total bottom had a remarkable penis, thick and long and veiny, like the living model for a sex toy. His foreskin rolled up and down over the head of his cock. I licked my fingers and put a couple in Winston's ass. The moment I did that, he ejaculated in huge spurts. Gregorio bent over and started licking the cum off Winston's belly. I said, "I guess it's time for another shower," but almost instantly, my friends stretched out and fell asleep. I lay down on Winston's right, Gregorio was on his left. I grabbed the top sheet and pulled it over us.

After dozing off for a bit, I awoke with a start and looked at the alarm clock. It was nearly seven, and we were expected at Frances's place for dinner. I woke up my friends, and we hastily got dressed. On the drive there, I said, "Well, that was fun. Let's do it again soon." Gregorio looked uncomfortable, and I knew not to continue the discussion.

We arrived in Newhall for dinner a little after 7:30. While Gregorio helped Frances with the preparations, Winston and I sat in the living room. As we stared at the television, I told him that I hoped that we could form our own threesome, away from the mainstream of the student body. I had noticed that people were avoiding us socially. When I pointed this out to Winston, he said,

"It is the story of my whole life. I am a misfit. Here, I tell people I am Albanian, and they say nothing."

I said, "They don't know what that means and don't want to risk being seen as ignorant. They hang out with people who are more or less like them."

"The habitual conformism of the American bourgeoisie. Look at their houses."

"I couldn't have said it better." I asked him, "Have you been speaking in class?"

"Not one word," he said.

"Do you have plans for Christmas?"

"No celebration. I am Muslim, or my family is—Bektashi. Our most religious ritual was slaughtering a goat at the end of Ramadan. Goat meat with yogurt sauce is delcious."

"My friend Moira wants me to house-sit for her over the Christmas break. It's a chance to get away from campus. Want to join me?"

Winston looked wistful and said, "Gregorio has asked me to visit him. I have never been to New Mexico."

I nodded and said, "Of course," trying not to show that I felt rejected. "Are you and he a couple?"

Winston thought for a moment and said, "If that is what he wants, I have no objection." I was caught off guard by such a noncommittal reply. He answered my inarticulate stammering. "Gregorio is very kind. I do not want to break his heart." He added, "I enjoy your jealousy. Really, men are so insecure." He laughed.

Before I could frame a response, Frances called us to dinner.

Over dessert, I turned to Winston and said, "I've been meaning to ask, how did you come to study in America? Or leave Albania in the first place?"

"Do you really care?" I nodded. "A long story, which I will try to shorten for you." He addressed all of us at the table: "I was born in Tirana, the capital. My family was very close to the center of power, never punished and no one purged. They repressed everything for the collective good, like proper socialists.

"Socialism in Albania was mainly the project of one man: Enver Hoxha, or 'the Guide,' as he wished to be called. Before I was born, he became all-powerful. But the power of a dictator does not extend to other countries. Foreigners did not care about the Albanians, with their strange culture and language. Hoxha transformed Albania into a tomb, a giant prison. No one was allowed to leave, and access to the outside world was limited. Only the elite studied foreign languages. In the 1980s, things changed. Hoxha was in poor health, and the West began to appear to us in images coming from across the Adriatic. It was illegal to watch the decadent Italian television programs, but everyone did so.

"After the death of Enver Hoxha, rivers of tears flowed, but there was happy news: Albania's isolation would come to an end. Embassies that were closed for many years opened again. My father had studied German and was appointed to the diplomatic mission to the DDR, *Deutsche Demokratische Republik*, or East Germany, as you Americans called it. He was allowed to take his family with him. When I was fourteen, we moved to East Berlin. My father was one of the most trusted men in the Albanian government, but far away from Tirana, his son had different ideas." Winston paused. "Father was terrified that I would do something to provoke the authorities and ruin everything. There was nothing to worry about, but his mentality was completely subservient to the Albanian government. We had diplomatic immunity, and the Stasi could not touch us."

Gregorio asked, "What's the Stasi?"

Winston took a long breath and reflected on how best to answer the question. "The *Staatssicherheitsdienst*, or State Security Service. It spied on everyone with a network of informers so large that by the end, the Stasi had accumulated files on six million people, or one-third of the population of the DDR." We looked at him with wide eyes, and he laughed. "I do not exaggerate. All documents were on paper, because computers were rudimentary in the East. There were so many files that the ground below Stasi Headquarters began to collapse under the weight of them. The secret center of power of the nation was sinking—a metaphor, if you wish to see it that way."

Winston turned and asked, "Understand now?" Gregorio nodded, and he continued, "In East Berlin, we received television and radio from the West. This changed my life completely. The second I heard punk music, my allegiance to Albania was finished. I looked around the city and saw others who loved punk. They dressed in a way no one imagined before. The police harassed them, but they continued to be defiant. It was thrilling. I joined them, hanging out and listening to music. I cut my hair and wore safety pins on my clothing. We looked stupid compared to punks who had done this in London or West Berlin ten years before, but we were the most radical people in the DDR.

"My father almost had a nervous breakdown. He was afraid that gossip about his crazy son was reaching Tirana. But our country was poor at this time, its economy was a disaster, and it needed every connection to rich countries. The DDR was rich compared to us. The few Albanians who spoke German were needed for diplomacy. A son who wore funny clothes meant nothing in this context.

"The DDR went through periods of openness or indifference, followed by brutal reaction. I discovered punk during an open period, then soon after, the state brought its fist down upon us." He paused and drew a breath. "I was lucky. A group of police grabbed me one night. They did not arrest me. They were drunk. I worried that they might beat me up, but they played a joke on me. Forced expatriation. No hearing, no phone call to my mother—they threw me out like a piece of trash. I saw that the Berlin Wall was not one wall but two, with a 'no man's land' in between them. I had heard rumors, but there it was in front of my face, this zone of tank traps and observation towers. For a moment I thought I would be killed.

"Then suddenly it was over. I found myself alone in West Berlin, with nothing but the clothes on my back. I went to the police, and they called an agency that took care of people who escaped from the DDR. I did not tell them I was Albanian. To them, I was only a punk, a type they had seen before, with no passport, only an identity card that stated my place of residence as East Berlin. My German was good enough that they did not question me. At that time, people from the East were given 'welcome money' and help with jobs and housing. I told the social worker assigned to me that I wanted to go to university, and this impressed her. With some pushing in the right places, I enrolled in the Freie Universität. This is where I studied when the Berlin Wall came down.

"At the end of the DDR, paranoia was everywhere, and some people did not believe what was happening. They thought it was a trick. During this time, I never called my family or wrote to them. A letter from the West caused trouble. When it was safe to take a trip to the East, I looked for my family. I learned that my father had a heart attack and died after I disappeared. He never knew what happened to his missing son." Tears were welling up in his eyes, but he continued, "My mother and sister moved back to Tirana to work as translators for a government that hardly existed, the last socialist system in Europe."

Frances asked, "Do you want a drink?"

"Please." She grabbed a can of beer from the refrigerator and handed it to Winston. He smiled. "In the East we had beer in bottles. An aluminum can was a sign that you were traveling to the West." He drank it with enthusiasm.

I asked, "Why are you called Winston?"

He laughed. "My punk name. I took it from Winston Smith in *1984*. No one I knew in East Berlin had read George Orwell, but we heard about his novel from television."

Frances asked, "What's your real name?"

"Andë, the word for 'desire' in ancient Illyrian. I cannot say how 'real' any Albanian name is. The fashions governing naming children in Albania changed from year to year. One generation received Turkish names, but this was seen as too Muslim, then Christian names became fashionable, but this was not tolerated very well in an atheist state. The safest names for members of the Party were Illyrian, from the 'pure' ancestors of the modern Albanians. But I think the Party invented them, as it invented our whole reality."

I asked, "When did you learn English?"

"I lived in the American Zone of Occupation. Learning English was easy. In East Berlin, my German was almost perfect. I was afraid that if I did not speak well, my father would punish me, or we would be called back to Albania. But in West Berlin, discipline was not so strict. No father. Therefore, I speak a funny kind of English, with this accent that no one can understand."

I said, "I love your accent."

"Racial fetishism!" Winston interjected, using an expression he had heard in one of the few critique classes he attended. We all laughed at this.

Frances asked, "When did you start painting?"

"I painted as a child in Albania, and a little in East Berlin. I was never interested in the official style of art. I dreamed about studying in England, like the punks, or in sunny California. I went to the Freie Universität to study English, but to do painting I needed to find another school. After surmounting many bureaucratic obstacles, I transferred to HdK, the Höchschule der Künste."

Gregorio asked an obvious question, "How can you afford to go to Cal Arts?"

"The great wealth of the Federal Republic of Germany. I have a special scholarship for studying art abroad. It does not allow me to live in luxury, but it pays for tuition and basic expenses. I got my education at the last moment before the prejudice against the *Ossis* became strong, and they imposed quotas on enrollment. With the stubbornness of a man of the Balkans, I got what I wanted. Every day in West Berlin, I heard someone shout *Ausländer raus!* Then I came to America, where nobody shouts racist shit at me in the street. What happens? People politely avoid me. They pretend I do not exist. Sometimes I prefer the Germans. At least they acknowledged my existence.

"Do you want to hear a joke?" We all nodded. "Ask an Austrian where the Balkans begin, and he says 'Slovenia'; ask a Slovenian where the Balkans begin, and he says 'Croatia'; the Croat will say Serbia; and the Serbians? Albania—they are not even Christian. But then go the other direction. The Germans will say, 'We are civilization and Austria and Hungary are already barbarians.' The French will tell you there is something dark and barbaric about Germany. Finally, the British position: all Europe is uncivilized; the Balkans begin at the English Channel."

It was a good joke, but there was only polite laughter, because the attitudes it described were unfamiliar to us.

Disappointed, Winston said, "Next time, I bring a map."

ELEVEN

At the beginning of Christmas break, I called Bernie and asked if he'd like to have dinner, and he said meekly, "I'm not sure I can afford it." I was surprised to hear this from someone who was not only my elder, but recently employed by the school I attended. I suggested he come over for tea instead, and I gave him Moira's address.

A couple of days later, I received a call from Gregorio. He told me he missed me and then put Winston on the line.

He said, "I see the real America now."

"What's it like?"

"Rather boring. We went to Albuquerque to shop for records. I like that city. Old Route 66 with the motels is how I thought all of America would look. Now I want to visit Las Vegas."

"You and every other European. How do you find staying with Gregorio's family?"

Winston lowered his voice. "They know nothing about us."

"Not that you two are together?" I asked, giving the last word a special emphasis.

"They think I am only his friend. No king size bed. He sleeps on a divan."

"Poor Gregorio. And his father is a therapist."

Winston added, "The father is very nice. Quiet. He likes basketball. I know nothing about it, but I am excused because I am a foreigner. He points to players from the former Yugoslavia for me to applaud. I do not correct him. The women in the family never stop talking. I understand very little. Spanish words about cooking, I think." He paused. "Mexican Christmas is nice. Tamales are delicious. I see now why Gregorio is a little bear."

There was a click as Gregorio picked up an extension. "Hey, we can't talk long. Are you in LA now?"

I said, "Yeah, I'm at my friend Moira's. It's not far from my old neighborhood."

Gregorio asked, "Do you want us to visit you on our way back?"

"Okay." I gave him the address. "When do you expect to be here?"

"We'll let you know."

∞

When Bernie came to see me, he seemed a bit shaken and walked with an obvious limp. I asked what was wrong, and after some hemming and hawing, he said, "Things have been difficult lately. I walked here." He sat down and took off his shoe. His sock was bloody. "I'm sorry, a blister must have burst."

I brought him a towel and tub of warm water and went looking for disinfectant and bandages. Bernie didn't appear very concerned, and I decided to take care of him. I bathed his foot and wrapped it. From the look of his wound, I guessed he was in quite a bit of pain.

I asked, "What happened to your car?"

"It's in the garage, but I don't know if I have the money to get it out. I may have to sell some things from the collection."

"Have you been working?"

"Barely. After Cal Arts, I managed to get a class at Otis, but the salary is so low I think I'd be better off on unemployment. Nobody warned me that adjunct faculty make almost nothing in California." I would have offered to lend him money if I hadn't been as poor as he was. He let out a sigh. "I never should have left New York. I gave up a rent-stabilized apartment in the East Village to take that job." He seemed to be on the verge of tears.

There was a knock at the door. It was Gregorio and Winston visiting as promised. They were clearly puzzled by Bernie's presence. I kissed them both, introduced them to my friend, and went to make tea. I said, "I thought you were going to give me some notice."

Gregorio called into the kitchen, "Sorry, we had trouble finding a pay phone."

I asked, "Did you drive non-stop?"

"No, we spent last night in Joshua Tree."

"It was beautiful, like another planet," Winston said with great enthusiasm.

Gregorio asked, "Is it okay if we take a shower?"

"Let me get you some towels." As I handed them to my friends, I said under my breath, "I wish I could join you."

Winston started to say something but Gregorio cut him off, "The desert is so dusty."

They took a suspiciously long time in the bathroom, then disappeared into the bedroom. I noticed sizable bulges under their towels, and Bernie couldn't keep from staring. Getting dressed took them a while, too. I wondered why they didn't wait until they got to Saugus to take a shower. Perhaps Gregorio wanted to rub his relationship with Winston in my face. Bernie said, "I see you've made some friends."

As I was about to respond, I heard a key turning in the lock of the front door. Moira and Temo came in. "Hello. I was wondering when you'd be back." I tried to say this loudly enough that the boys in the bedroom would hear me.

Moira came over and gave me a hug. "I called, but maybe you didn't hear the message."

"I have my hands full at the moment."

Gregorio and Winston appeared, looking (to me, at least) like lovers who had just had sex. Temo was immediately drawn to my friends. He asked, "Aren't you going to introduce us?" I reminded Temo that he had met Gregorio the day I moved into my studio, and they both got sour looks on their faces. Winston waved from across the room.

It was decided that we'd eat at Don Felix. A look of panic came over Bernie until Moira said, "Dinner's on us. Happy New Year." As we walked down the hill, Moira sidled up to me and whispered, "Is Bernie okay?"

"Not really," I answered. "But to be honest, I haven't heard the whole story yet. Money problems."

Moira nodded and said, "Maybe he can take a couple of shifts at Libros Revolución."

"Good idea."

Before we were seated, Moira had a quiet word with Bernie, and his mood improved. He said very little that evening, preferring to observe the interactions of the people present, most of whom he didn't know.

Dinner conversation was tentative and rather strained. The only high point came when we expressed our unanimous admiration for the song "All Cats Are Grey" by The Cure. Temo's presence seemed to inhibit everyone. He glowered at me from time to time as a warning that I shouldn't talk about our affair. He had nothing to worry about, because I had little desire to explain it to anyone. Winston took an immediate and visible dislike to him. When Temo excused himself to go to the men's room, Winston whispered to me, "That man is a spy."

"How can you tell?" I asked a bit skeptically.

"Something is wrong." He asked me, "Have you fucked him?" I hesitated, and he immediately said, "Your face says you have. Be careful around him. If you are lucky, you will get nothing more than a case of the clap."

Temo came out of the toilet and, noticing that Winston and I were in a private conversation, shot us a brief, cutting glance without anyone else seeing. Winston elbowed me in the ribs as if to say, "See, I knew he was trouble," then turned his attention to Gregorio.

When we returned to the apartment, I quickly went back to the bedroom, which was very stuffy, opened the windows, and stripped the bed. I carried the sheets, towels, and Bernie's socks down to the building's laundry room and started washing them. I came back upstairs to find Gregorio and Winston about to leave. Moira handed them Libros Revolución cards and they thanked her. I told Gregorio it would take me a while to get ready, and he mentioned something about having no room in his truck.

Moira offered, "I can drive you back to campus. And Bernie, I'm guessing you're on the way." He nodded.

Gregorio announced, "I want a picture." He took out a digital camera and tripod that his parents had given him for Christmas, set the timer, and motioned for us to stand closer to each other. He bounded into the frame, and hopped back out to get one more photo of the group without him. Then he and Winston left.

After I made Moira's bed and gathered my things, I told her, "Thanks for everything. If I had stayed in my studio over Christmas break, I would have gone nuts."

"It was totally fine. Any time."

We went out the door, and Temo held me back and whispered, "Email me." He decided to ride along as Moira took me up to campus, but he said nothing until after Moira dropped Bernie off at his apartment. Temo probably wanted to gossip about my friends, and to prevent me from talking to Moira about him behind his back. As soon as Bernie left the car, he asked, "Are Winston and Gregorio a couple?"

"Yes. Isn't it obvious?"

"They looked affectionate." Temo turned to me in the back seat and asked, "Where is Winston from?"

"Albania, by way of Germany." I remembered what Winston had told me in the restaurant, and I kept my answer brief.

"Suspicious," he said. I laughed to myself, because the feelings of distrust were mutual. "You like him, don't you?" Temo asked.

I blushed, but it was too dark in the car for anyone to see. "I like them both very much. I wondered if maybe I could join them in a threesome."

Temo laughed cruelly, and I immediately regretted confiding such an intimate detail to him. He said, "Three-ways never work. There's always a favorite."

"That would be Winston," I said sadly.

Moira asked, "Isn't there anyone else for you at school?"

"No. I sometimes wonder if I've become a priest."

Temo laughed again, less cruelly this time. "In my experience, celibacy is the exception rather than the rule among priests."

Moira exclaimed, "You men all have one thing on your minds!"

"No, three things: cock, ass, and cunt. In what order depends on the man." Temo had a sly expression on his face. I rolled my eyes, but Moira remained unaware, as she was concentrating on driving. The area where the Hollywood Freeway and I-5 merged was uncharacteristically crowded at that hour. Temo said smugly, "If you ask me, you could do better than a Chicano faggot and a smelly refugee from the Balkans."

Moira snapped at him, "*¿Cómo te atreves?*" She shook her head in disgust. "*!Y te llamas izquierdista!*"

"I've been meaning to ask, are you *really* a leftist, Temo?"

He paused for a moment and said, "Leftists always lose, even when they win. They want to make a better world, even if they have to kill everyone to do it."

"So that would be a 'no.' What a poser." I added, "For your information, that 'Chicano faggot,' as you call him, bears more of a resemblance to an actual human being than anyone else at that school. And Winston is a real punk."

"You must be joking. Punk is dead, *payaso*."

In a tone of mock innocence, I asked, "Temo, you sound a little jealous. Are you offering me a *fresa*?"

He snorted, "You wish."

Moira huffed, "I thought you two were getting along so well. Temo, you should make an effort. He's my oldest friend."

I stared at Temo, and he stared back. Unseen by Moira, he pursed his lips. He turned to her and said, "I'm only teasing, *blanca*," as the car pulled up to the front entrance of the school.

∞

Winston, Gregorio, and I chose similar course schedules for spring semester so we would at least have each other's company in class. We met Frances at registration, and she greeted us warmly. A person we hadn't seen before was with her. "Gentlemen, this is Carmen."

"Hello," we said in unison. Carmen had a buzz cut dyed vermilion. She wore large, clunky earrings and bracelets. Her lipstick was dark purple, a shade that Chicana homegirls used to wear, and it accentuated her pouty lips. She opened her mouth and out came a stream of words barely intelligible over the noise of registration, and delivered in a thick New York accent. She said that she'd just returned from a semester in Glasgow, and for an instant, it seemed that she slipped into a Scottish brogue. I had trouble forming any definite impression of this woman. All I knew was that Frances was enamored of her, so I kept any doubts to myself.

I asked Frances, "When is your thesis show scheduled?"

She said, "I got last pick, so it's early, before spring break. That reminds me, I want to do a portrait of the three of you. I need to take pictures for reference. Then you can do sittings individually in my studio." Gregorio and Winston had wandered off by then.

I asked, "Nude or fully clothed?"

She got a devilish look in her eye. "They wouldn't pose in the nude for me."

"Maybe if you asked nicely. I want to see how you'd paint Winston's legs. They're so hairy that he looks like a centaur."

Frances thought for a moment and said, "We could do a mythological scene. That would really annoy the faculty."

It took some convincing to get Winston and Gregorio to pose for Frances, but she wouldn't take no for an answer. She photographed us after dinner and drinks at her place. Winston got a rock hard erection as soon as we stripped off our clothes. He was more of an exhibitionist than I realized, and posed exactly like a satyr in a classical statue. Frances ran out of film and retired to her bedroom to rewind the roll. It was black and white, a choice that meant it could be developed on campus and not censored or destroyed by a local drugstore. Probably imagining that we would be fucking, she stayed in her bedroom for a while. Gregorio and I watched Winston jerk off until he lost his erection. Soon afterwards, Frances came out and announced dessert. We ate peach cobbler in our underwear.

∞

One day Winston said to me, "You are a writer. Perhaps you can fix something I am trying to write. My English is not good enough. I have some notes."

"What's it about?"

"The American Dream."

For a couple of days, I worked on the notes that Winston gave me, and I came up with the following text:

> In de-industrialized America, the proletariat is about ninety per cent of the population. Proletarians do not acknowledge this; instead they call themselves middle class. They believe they are in control of democratic institutions because of their superior numbers, but real power lies in the hands of the super-rich, the spiritual descendants of the Four Hundred Families of the Gilded Age.
>
> The super-rich live above the law and respect only themselves. Below them in the social order is the bourgeoisie, consisting of people who live comfortably with money made from what the English once called the learned professions—medicine, law, academia—or if they lack the necessary degrees, finance and advertising. In objective economic terms, this professional class has only two functions: first, to occupy real estate that appreciates in value, and second, to provide a conduit through which the super-rich extract surplus labor from the proletariat. Their existence is completely devoid of any other purpose, so in their aimlessness, they have claimed for themselves the role of arbiters. They control American culture—not its material aspects, which are in the hands of monopoly capital, but its ideological aspects. They serve as a maternal presence, kindly but sternly enforcing standards of propriety by contributing to charity, limiting the sale of guns, supporting the arts, generally abstaining from rape and theft, and above all, making sure that no one disregards class distinctions. They profess the most liberal politics—some of them even claim to be radicals—but the real circumstances of their lives tell a different story.

As the American dream of upward mobility is revealed to be impossible and the social relations of production become ever more parasitic, bourgeois professionals struggle to maintain their status. They do so by evicting the poor from public space, limiting the proletariat's access to public education, and intimidating all who will listen with the specialized jargon they learned as undergraduates and hear regurgitated in the news media. They help the super-rich steal with obscene impunity, yet at the same time, they protest against racism, sexism, homophobia, the death penalty, and environmental destruction, all the while blaming the proletariat for being ignorant and reactionary.

The professional classes collaborate with the super-rich in the unspoken hope that one day they will be able to ascend in the social order and join the blessed. They never will.

I handed the edited version to Winston, and he read it with excitement. "You did well. Now what do we do with it?"

"Let's make a video."

"What images will we use?" Winston asked.

"I know what I want to shoot, the construction of Santa Clarita. It's the largest 'master planned' community in Los Angeles County. The area is owned by the Newhall family, who bought an entire Spanish *rancho* in the nineteenth century. By the way, their descendant Beaumont wrote the standard history of photography used in art schools everywhere. The kind of social engineering you wrote about…"

Winston interrupted, "*We* wrote about. I cannot write that way."

"This social engineering is coming into existence all around us. A stretch of desert and a freeway off-ramp became a city of a quarter million people in twenty-five years. And Cal Arts was the first stage. We are part of the master plan."

Over the next few days, Gregorio drove us to the edges of construction sites to shoot views of giant rows of houses. The construction techniques employed were extremely efficient and resembled a production line, but one where the workers instead of the objects manufactured did the moving. The drainage systems handling irrigation water for grass and trees resembled the giant monuments of ancient civilizations. Perhaps one day people would marvel at the ruins of these modern earthworks and puzzle over their function. We encountered no resistance to shooting the locations; indeed, some of them were so deserted that we wondered how the residents could avoid going insane from social isolation. Workers living in these places endured commutes that often lasted two hours or more, listening to books on tape or relishing the time away from screaming children and demanding spouses. I began to think that Winston's narration, which I found unsparing and dogmatic on first reading, wasn't harsh enough.

The tone of Winston's writing reminded me of *der schwarze Kanal* (the Black Channel), an East German response to West German news broadcasts. Written by Karl-Eduard von Schnitzler, the episodes reedited and acerbically ridiculed the original sources in language so extreme that only a miniscule audience cared to watch. The program was an example of the most rebarbative leftist culture appealing only to connoisseurs of the perverse. It amused me to think of unleashing this on our fellow students.

In the studio, we recorded two versions of the voice over and decided mine was better for editing. It would also be easier for viewers to understand, even if Winston, as the original author of the text, gave a more emphatic reading. The final video was a little less than five minutes long, including the titles. Winston used his punk surname for his credit.

∞

We first showed our video, called *American Dream*, in a critique class taught by a well-meaning but ineffectual instructor who hadn't had an exhibition since the late-1970s in San Francisco. To hear her tell it, her main artistic subject was "the cultural construction of masculinity," but this was difficult to discern in the art that, from all indications, she had ceased to make around 1982. We figured this instructor would at least have the virtue of being easily offended. She and her students were exactly the sort of people we hoped to reach.

While criticizing the built environment of Santa Clarita had been a commonplace for decades at Cal Arts (which was no architectural gem, either), we were unsure whether our audience would recognize themselves in our text. We needn't have worried, because when we showed the video, many protestations followed. The class sounded like a gaggle of Baptist ministers caught *in flagrante delicto* with male prostitutes. Winston and I could barely contain our pleasure.

The instructor said one thing of use to us: Winston Smith, the name of Orwell's protagonist, had already been taken as a pseudonym by the artist who designed record covers for the Dead Kennedys. News of this had failed to reach an Albanian punk in East Berlin. There followed a discussion of John Heartfield, the great anti-Nazi collage artist, who chose to live in the East after the war. His work had little to do with our video, but the topic gave Winston a chance to give a short lecture about the culture of his adopted country, the German Democratic Republic, which had ceased to exist a few years after he moved there. He explained that the phrase *der schwarze Kanal* could be translated not only as the Black Channel but also as "sewer pipe." The instructor, who wagged a pedantic finger at his sense of irony, was nonetheless impressed that he had a special body of knowledge of which the other students were ignorant. That evening, we changed his credit on the video to read simply "Winston."

Over the next few days, Gregorio, Winston and I noticed the students keeping their distance, and we got the impression that they were talking about us. Frances confirmed that this was indeed the case. I was upset by the gossip at first, but Gregorio, a Smiths fan always ready with a quip from Oscar Wilde, said triumphantly, "There is only one thing in the world worse than being talked about, and that is not being talked about."

∞

After showing *American Dream* a few more times, Winston went back to painting. He always worked with his canvases facing away from his studio door, and he didn't let people see anything he considered unfinished. Gregorio continued to work on his miniature gouaches, while I became the video artist, a distinction I didn't relish, in light of the examples of the genre I had seen in classes.

I had decided not to take Post Studio Art in the spring semester, so my Fridays were free. I could stay as late as I wished at the Thursday night parties, more frequent now that students were installing exhibitions every week. I rarely woke up before noon the next day, but I had enough time to get ready, have lunch, then sit in on Thom Andersen's Film Today class. It was wonderful to see films projected in the Bijou, the main theater on campus. The only aspect I disliked was the presence of so many pets in the auditorium. Why did people need these creatures to accompany them everywhere? I once had the unforgettable experience of watching *The Death of Empedocles*, directed by Jean-Marie Straub and Danièle Huillet; the sound of actors reciting Friedrich Hölderlin's verse in the Italian countryside was accompanied by the sound of dogs licking their balls.

TWELVE

As spring break approached, Frances was preoccupied with having as much sex as possible with Carmen and preparing her thesis exhibition. She planned to include her giant portrait of Gena Rowlands in the show, and on the opposite wall, the painting of Gregorio, Winston, and me. Each of us had sat for hours in Frances's studio. She didn't prevent her subjects from moving around and talking, since conversation contributed to how she executed a likeness. She also painted us in pairs and observed the dynamics between us. At times I felt as though I was taking part in a psychological experiment.

Once, when it was just the two of us alone in the studio, I asked her about Carmen. She waxed ecstatic about her girlfriend. "Did you know she has a pierced tongue?"

I smiled. "Somehow that escaped my notice."

"She reads to me in bed, and it's really hot. *Kathy Goes to Haiti* is like a sex toy for us."

I said, "I don't know that book. I must check it out."

"I met Kathy Acker once, but she didn't seem interested in me at all. I babbled like an idiot, so who can blame her? Anyway, Carmen is much more fun. I finally found a girl whose mouth spouts theory *and* eats my pussy!" We both doubled over in laughter.

Frances didn't let us see the painting until it was nearly done. We gathered in her studio for the unveiling, and we all gasped when we saw it. The painting showed us full figure in the nude against a vibrant yellow background. On the left, Gregorio held his hands behind his back. He gazed at the face of Winston, standing in the center with his eyes closed and his head cocked at an angle. Winston's right arm rested on Gregorio's shoulder, while his left arm was bent with his hand grazing his own shoulder in a sinuous, stylized pose. I stood on the right. I gazed at the two lovingly, as though I wanted to join my friends but couldn't. Because I was the tallest of the three, my eyes were downcast. Both Gregorio and I had enigmatic smiles on our faces. Winston's face betrayed little emotion, but the enormous hard-on between his legs suggested what he was thinking.

On the wall of Frances's studio I saw the image that served as the basis of the painting's composition. It was an early twentieth century photograph of three Sicilian peasant boys in whom the photographer, Wilhelm von Gloeden, saw an ideal of antiquity. They stood against an old whitewashed wall bathed in direct sunlight. The shadow of the camera encroached upon the lower edge of the picture. I knew nothing about these youths, and only a little more about von Gloeden, whose works were destroyed in great numbers by the Italian fascists. His photographs, at once heartfelt and creepy, occupy an uncertain place in the history of their medium. Often dismissed as kitsch, they represent Sicily, an island unchanged for centuries yet on the verge of modernity, filtered through the imagination of an aristocratic German aesthete yearning for the simplicity and freedom of a mythological place—the South, the ancient past—where he could be at ease with his desire for male flesh.

∞

Douglas Crimp came to give a lecture and do studio visits that week. He was widely regarded as an eminence in art theory, having co-edited *October* and written an essay for the journal with the fetching title "On the Museum's Ruins." Though trained as an art historian, he had increasingly turned his attention to politics. I had met the man once by chance a few years before, and I expected him to be serious and intimidating. Somewhat to my surprise his entire conversation revolved around two topics: the White Party, an annual drug-fueled gathering of urban gay men, and shopping.

Crimp's talk focused exclusively on AIDS activism, and he provoked the audience when he asked, "Do you want to paint bowls of fruit for the rest of your life, or do you want to make a difference?" He was either completely ignorant of what art students had been doing for the last few decades, or he wanted to pose his question in the most insulting way, comparing us to hobbyists painting along with Bob Ross on television. Winston very loudly got up from his chair and stormed out the door. After the lecture, I found him in his studio feverishly at work. He was making as many paintings as he could before the meeting he would have with Crimp.

By the next afternoon, small studies in gouache on paper littered Winston's studio. They all depicted bowls of fruit, with the phrase "Make a Difference" like an advertising slogan wrapping around the composition in a circle. I couldn't resist the urge to eavesdrop on the ensuing conversation. The laugh I hoped to hear never came. The visitor couldn't take a joke. Then Winston showed his real work, paintings I hadn't seen, with the exception of the exquisite portrait of Enver Hoxha. I heard Crimp ask primly, "Is this some sort of tribute? Are you taking these dictators seriously, or is this another joke, like the bowls of fruit?"

There was a long pause, and I heard the rustling of papers. Insecure about his English in an environment where incessant discussion held sway, Winston felt the need for a prepared text. He began talking, half reading and half extemporizing: "The assumption behind your questions is that if my attitude towards these men and the social system they represent is ironic, then I am subversive. If I take them seriously, I am conformist. But now I live under capitalism. The capitalist system has as its inherent condition of functioning that its own ideology must *not* be taken seriously. Cynicism is the prevailing mode of ideology today. The ideal political subject is one who has ironic distance from the system. Therefore, the only way to be really subversive is *not* to develop critical distance or irony at all, but precisely to take the system more seriously than it takes itself. I am presenting you with icons of defunct state religions, and I dare you to worship them."

There was a minor commotion in response to this statement. It occurred to me that Winston was the very opposite of the proper art school queer who talked about politics all the time but never accomplished anything, and talked about sex while getting none. He also refused to heed the exhortations to have "safer sex," but he never whined in self-justification, either. When the conversation turned to this subject, Winston could take no more and bellowed, "Why be a good boy? They kill you in the end anyway, even if you act like a virgin. Be a bad boy! Get fucked every day, and have fun!"

Crimp suddenly left the studio, ducking slightly, as though he was avoiding a volley of turds thrown at him. We ran into each other in the courtyard, and he gave me a look that indicated he had seen Frances's triple portrait of us earlier in the day. He shook his head with distaste. As I entered the studio, Winston shouted after him, "AIDS vampire!" He turned to me and said calmly, "These people who call themselves postmodernists are like a horse's ass, producing only shit."

Once inside, I gazed at the paintings I hadn't seen before: portraits of Lenin and Stalin, approximately life size, and radiating a chaotic intensity. Winston had achieved a new level of proficiency and finesse with the technique he had started using for the Hoxha portrait, which was hidden away. Spatters and violent strokes of a palette knife recalled abstract expressionism, but from these marks emerged famous faces that, once recognized, brought each painting into sharp focus. The subjects looked wizened and covered with blemishes. His work emphasized the faults that retouchers were at pains to remove from official portraits. I stood in awe and asked, "Are these two from this semester?" He nodded. "They're amazing. I heard what you said about them. Excuse me for listening, but it was too good to ignore."

"A bourgeois American can pretend that these images never existed, or that they are irrelevant now, but I live with them in my head. What sort of kitsch does this self-righteous fool want from a painter? To me, Bill Clinton looks like a piece of chewed-up bubble gum. Shall I paint AIDS patients with faces like Christian saints?"

I continued to examine the paintings and asked, "Are you working from photos?"

"There is no need. I saw these faces every day before I came to the West. You must remember, history arrived late on the other side of the Berlin Wall. I am the 'other' that these art world ghouls talk about, abject and ignored, an inconvenient reminder and an impediment to 'progress.' Fuck you all." Winston looked agitated. Thinking it would calm him down, I hugged him, but he didn't want to be consoled and wrenched himself away.

∞

I left Winston's studio and took a walk around campus. I ended up in the library, where I sat at a computer. I typed an email address, bolsillodepayaso@aol.com, and a message: "Temo, How are you? This is my first email. Congratulate me on entering the twentieth century shortly before it ends. Are you busy next week? I will be on spring break. I can take a train to Los Angeles and meet you some time if you want." I had heard that apostrophes made words look like gobbledygook in emails to recipients on a different computer platform, so I refrained from using contractions, just as Winston did when he spoke. I wondered if my message sounded like Winston. I had been hanging out with him a lot, even ghost writing for him, and it wouldn't have surprised me. I added, "How is your hole?" in case he wondered who I was or why I was emailing him. I hit send and hoped I had spelled the address correctly.

I looked at the messages in my inbox, all of them useless, and as I did, Temo's response came: "I work on Tuesdays and Wednesdays until four. Call the store from Union Station when you arrive. P. S. My hole needs an expert to wreck it." I started to get an erection. I adjusted myself and typed a brief response, then logged off.

Having done this, I walked back to the Annex. On my way, I saw Frances and Carmen walking arm in arm. Frances asked, "Are you coming to the opening tomorrow night?"

"I wouldn't miss it for the world." They both smiled.

∞

Before the party began, I had to attend my Thursday critique class. As it happened, Carmen was showing her work that day. I wondered if this was a coincidence, or if she had scheduled her critique to compensate for Frances being the center of attention later. Attention was like a drug to which many art students were addicted. If Carmen got a fix that afternoon, she wouldn't be tempted to pull any stunts at Frances's opening. I expected the usual Cal Arts dreck: sketchy, slapdash work supported by an elaborate theoretical apparatus. Carmen did not disappoint in this regard, as the piece she showed imitated Allen Ruppersberg's work consisting of the entire text of Oscar Wilde's *The Picture of Dorian Gray* hand written in ballpoint pen on canvases. Her technique was identical, but the chosen text was Charlotte Perkins Gilman's "The Yellow Wallpaper." She had made a wise choice, as the story was published about a year after Wilde's novel, and historical comparison was possible, in the event that anyone noticed the work's resemblance to its predecessor. It was also less than one-tenth the length of Ruppersberg's marathon copying of Wilde, therefore something that she could knock off in a single night.

Carmen began the discussion, "Often I use material I don't understand. I read something and I say, 'I don't believe that, what's going on?' The way I find out is to copy it, word for word. The story intrigued me. It's about a woman who cracks up and goes on a rest cure. She stays in a room that has yellow wallpaper and bars on the windows. It's all done for her own good supposedly, but it's like she's in a prison."

It was a brilliant first gambit. Carmen put everyone on their guard against sexism, while at the same time declaring a kind of modesty—I don't understand—and leaving unmentioned the relation of her work to that of the man who had the idea first.

She went on to describe her alienation, "I hate my mother. But I also hate my fathers, you know, the people who taught me. I do exactly what they told me not to. I feel our culture is an imposition. In school it's always 'great culture'—this is how you should think, this is a great work of art—it's the same in the art world. Of course, these great works are all made by white men. They don't have anything to do with me. I mean, it's that feeling of this might be great, but if there's no meaning for me, and it doesn't relate to my life, what do I care?"

There was an undeniable narcissism in her statement—I felt like asking, "Isn't it important to experience things that don't relate directly to one's own life, in order to learn how other people think?"—but at the same time, I was beginning to warm up to this woman, who had clearly thought a lot about these questions.

The class curmudgeon asked, "Why make work that illustrates some theory?" The question, while appropriate, was intended to dampen the mood. He believed anyone staking out a position in a critique class deserved to be punished, or at the very least brought down to earth and made every bit as unhappy and unproductive as he was.

Completely unfazed by this man's attempt to piss on her, Carmen, who excelled at thinking on her feet, had the last word: "I get bored of hearing myself scream. I get bored with the sound of my own voice. It's about whether you have a few possibilities or lots of possibilities. And those systems of whatever—journalism, art, schooling, where the possibilities are narrowed and narrowed— that's what I'm against. You know, against rigidity of meaning. I'm against a fixed identity or image." As often happened, at the moment someone said something truly worthy of discussion, it was time for the class to be dismissed. I was disappointed that Carmen didn't deliver the critique that seemed to be latent in her final sentence. It had been a few years since identity politics was a relevant idea in the upper reaches of the art world, but nothing convincing had taken its place, unless one counted an anodyne concept like "beauty," which I didn't, since it had about as much intellectual heft as an auction catalogue. As far as I was concerned, the beautiful, in the sense of that which is pleasing, was merely the lie that a society told itself in order to conduct business as usual.

∞

When I arrived at Frances's opening, the festivities were just getting underway. I was surprised to see that Paul had come to congratulate Frances. I decided to be civil and approached him cautiously. He gave me a big hug and said, "A three-way relationship with a couple of my former tricks… not bad, my dear."

"Bitch."

"Oh, I'm just playing," he said. "Really, that painting is quite a triumph. I hope everyone is well and truly terrified of you."

"I believe so." Carmen and Frances waved at Paul, and I asked, "Do you know them well?"

"Frances used to be my closest friend, that is, until I stole from her. I was a wild child in those days." He looked at me and corrected himself, "Or wilder than I am now. Anyway, her lovely companion is a piece of work."

I raised an eyebrow and asked, "What do you know?"

"Hold on, momma needs a nip before telling that little tale." He took a swig of whatever tipple was powering his stream of palaver. "Carmen, named after the opera by Miss Bizet, has a different story for every listener. She tailors her approach to the tastes and interests of her mark." I looked a bit incredulous. "Yes, I said it, mark. She's a con artist *par excellence*. I'd give her a wide berth, darling, unless you want every idea you've ever had appropriated and claimed as her own."

"Isn't plagiarism her artistic strategy, as it were?"

He snorted. "Oh it is, but she admits that only when she's called on it."

"I had a class with her today. She seemed pretty smart, and we had a good conversation."

He said, "There's definitely something going on inside that noggin, don't get me wrong. She went to San Francisco Art Institute, where she studied with none other than Kathy Acker, the avatar of postmodern literature herself."

I said, "That's where the leopard print leggings come from."

"Now you've clocked her. Within a few days of meeting Acker, she started going to the same stores and buying the wardrobe. Makeup and tattoos, too, natch. I never inquired about the pierced labia, for obvious reasons. She really started 'Eve-ing' Miss Acker." Paul checked to see if I understood the reference to *All About Eve* and its thinly veiled lesbian drama of a young aspirant pouring herself all over the aging diva she wishes to replace. Satisfied that I was catching his drift, he continued, "Carmen started walking, talking, and fucking like her idol, until even Acker, who normally yearns for devoted imitators to join her entourage, became unnerved. Carmen needed to get out of Frisco, since the queen bee was onto her scam, so she came here. She's continuing her Acker routine, I see, probably because there's no one around worthy of imitation. This kind of vampire needs a famous woman who's become a parody of herself to glom onto. Broad strokes, cunty, broad strokes."

I asked, "Do you think she has a personality underneath all the affectations?"

"Probably, but in her heart of hearts, she's afraid that she'll bore us with it." Carmen, ever vigilant about what people thought of her, shot us a quick glance, icy and a bit cruel, as if to say, I know you're talking about me. "Let's go for a walk," Paul suggested. When Frances and Carmen started to make out vigorously, we found the exit. As we left, he said one more thing, "In case you wondered, there's a trust fund. She hates mommy and daddy, but while they're still alive, she has to talk to them so they don't cut her off." As we walked, Paul asked, "Would you do a gin-sodden old thing a favor? I'm way too drunk to drive. Do you have room on your humble futon tonight?"

"Yes, as long as you keep your hands to yourself."

"We're sisters, I promise."

The next morning Paul slipped out very early to avoid running into Winston and Gregorio, who had kept a low profile at Frances's opening. I got up late and looked around for them. I hoped they hadn't left for spring break without saying goodbye. I returned to find a note: "Sorry we missed you. See you in a week. XO, Gregorio & Winston." I didn't expect them to take me along, although I did fantasize about instigating a bit of trouble in their relationship, a ploy that probably would have pleased Winston.

I often thought about our three-way in Gregorio's house, and I wondered if such a thing would ever happen again.

∞

On Tuesday I knocked on Frances's door to see if she could drive me to the Newhall train station, which was only a few blocks from her apartment. Instead I found Carmen, who told me she could give me a ride. In the car on the way there, she asked me if I'd be in a video, something based upon Clarice Lispector, the celebrated Brazilian writer. She planned to start production after spring break. No memorization would be required, and I'd get a script in a week's time. For all the doubts Paul sowed in my mind, I had to admit that Carmen seemed quite competent. There's something to be said for getting things done, I thought.

∞

On the train, I trimmed and filed my nails, and when I arrived at Union Station, I called Libros Revolución. Temo answered and said he could be ready in an hour. I killed time on Olvera Street, then took the subway to Westlake. I got to the store a little early. He turned the sign to "Closed" and locked the front door. I asked if that was a problem, and he said, "We have no customers at this hour."

We went to the back room, where he had spread a drop cloth on a mattress. The room reeked of piss, but by that point I was so horny I hardly cared. We both took off our clothes and began kissing. I got hard almost immediately, and he sucked me off as I lay on the mattress. He had acquired some skills (and completely gotten rid of his gag reflex) since I saw him last. I complimented him on his technique, and he said, "I'm getting better as a whore. Look at my ass." He flipped over, and I could hardly believe what I saw. His hole resembled a deep canyon with jagged edges around the rim.

"What the hell have you done?"

He said, "I've been busy. Crisco is on the desk."

I grabbed the can and wondered what his fellow employees must have thought he was doing with it. Perhaps he had stashed it, like the mattress, in a special hiding place. I went to the bathroom and washed my hands thoroughly, like a surgeon preparing for an operation, except I didn't put on a pair of gloves. I spread the Crisco on my right hand and probed his hole as he lay on all fours. I felt little resistance. It was as though my hand simply fell into his ass. I pulled out and greased up the rest of my arm. Within minutes, I was inside him up to my elbow. He exhaled sharply and said, "Deeper." I had never gone that deep in an ass, and I hesitated. Offering direction, he said, "Turn left," and I plunged deeper still. My elbow irritated his rectum, and my arm started getting bloodier than I expected. I pulled out as quickly as I could, and he shuddered violently. He let out a moan reminding me of something on a Halloween sound effects record. He continued to shudder in the throes of a full-body orgasm for several minutes. He finally collapsed in a lump, exhausted, on the mattress. After a pause, he said, "That was amazing." I lay down next to him and we kissed. It was now dusk, and the store was supposed to be closed. He looked at the watch still on his wrist and said, "*Coño*, there's a meeting here in fifteen minutes." I helped him put things away as quickly as possible. I did what I could to get the grease off my arm with dishwashing liquid and salt, but it still stunk of shortening and felt greasy. We got dressed, and Temo opened the door to the shop and turned on the lights just in time for the first arrivals at the meeting. He spoke to a couple of people in Spanish, some things I could barely hear, then came to see me. He said, "Let's go out the back way."

He told me not to touch his car with greasy hands as he drove us to Moira's. He had a key to her place and explained, "Sometimes she asks me to open her apartment for meetings while she works late. I know her schedule very well. She returns tonight at midnight." As he opened the door, he said, "We can take a shower here."

I found a pair of towels and turned on the water in the shower. I waited for it to warm up and watched Temo undress in the weak light of the living room as I took off my clothes. His body was sleek and toned and slightly hairier than I remembered. He looked as nearly perfect as I could imagine. He joined me in the shower and smiled. He poured shampoo on my arm and scrubbed it until it was degreased. He began to get an erection. I looked down, and he cleared his throat, as if to say "not for you." He turned around and began to grind his ass into my crotch. I got hard again and he positioned his hole over my engorged cock. I barely noticed that it was inside him, because his ass was so loose. He said, "I have a real clown's pocket now." I pulled out and jerked off. When I was about to come, he knelt down and swallowed my load. We held each other for a moment in the steamy shower. Then he said, "I'm hungry. Let's have dinner."

My stomach growled. "Yeah, I'm hungry, too." It occurred to me that I had lost track of time. It was dark outside, so it could have been any time between seven and eleven at night, or even later.

He got out of the shower, wiped off the mirror, and began to comb his hair, an operation that took a fairly long time. He gathered his clothes and put them on piece by piece, and found his watch, which had slid down next to the sink. Then he sat on the toilet and groaned like an animal expelling afterbirth. He quickly closed the lid of the toilet and said, "Don't look in there," as he flushed it. He washed his ass in Moira's sink, and dried it off with a hand towel. He placed it back on the rack. I gave him a disapproving look, and he said, "I'll do laundry later."

We ate dinner almost in silence, and it became clear to me that although we shared a great sexual rapport, we had nothing much in common. I hardly noticed this before, because we often had conversations with Moira present. He did his best to make small talk, but we finished quickly then got in the car. Once we were alone, he finally opened up. "I could be in love with a man like you. You know my body inside and out. I'll be your sex slave, your pussy. Do you want that?"

"I think so. But I'm not sure I trust you."

He grunted, "*I'm* the one who has to trust *you*." He glanced in my direction with a look I couldn't read. "Just remember that if you want a real bottom, I'm here. You can put anything you want in my cunt. You can whore me out and watch the whole neighborhood fuck my sloppy ass, too."

"Aren't you afraid of AIDS?"

He snorted and laughed. "Who cares? They have the best medicines now. And Moira must have told you, my family is rich. In America, I'll live to be an old man shitting in my diaper."

I found his attitude reprehensible, and at the same time, completely logical. Healthcare in the US was made for entitled brats like him. If that Clinton fool hadn't signed the Defense of Marriage Act, I could have married the guy, sharing his wealth and health insurance, living like a hedonistic faggot, as he no doubt would have called me. The thought of all this made me uncomfortable, though I didn't let on, and he continued to talk about the sex life we could share.

I let my attention wander for a bit, but came back to the conversation when he said, "I'm serious, *payaso*."

"Don't call me that," I said emphatically. I could hardly wait to get out of the car, but at the same time, I admired his fanaticism. Would he ever find someone to live up to his ideal? Would he introduce this person to his family? I had many questions that I knew would not receive answers. Perhaps he'd never know the answers himself.

He accompanied me to my studio, and once we were inside, we kissed. He said, "You're a thoroughly despicable American, but I love you."

"You know how to charm a guy, don't you?"

I hugged him tightly and suddenly felt inspired. I licked his neck at its most sensitive spot and started to give him a hickey. He pulled away and said, "No marks."

"Do you want to sleep here tonight?" I asked.

"Yes, but my parents are expecting me at home."

I said, "You didn't mean it when you said 'I love you,' did you?"

"You'll never know," he said with a smirk on his face, As he left, he turned around and looked at me in a way that made me think he really did love me. Perhaps the dim light of the studio was playing tricks, or he was. Temo left and I didn't go after him, though a part of me wanted to grab him and declare my love.

THIRTEEN

I waited out the rest of spring break in a foul mood. I wanted to talk to Bernie, and when I finally reached him, he seemed in good spirits. He said, "I've decided to move back to New York. The goal is to do it over the summer."

I responded right away, "I'll miss you."

"There's always email. You have an account, right?"

"I started using it only last week." I could hear Bernie laughing on the other end of the line. "I guess Los Angeles didn't really work out for you. How is your car running?"

He said, "It needs more repairs before I can drive it cross-country. I'm saving up for that. I can't afford to buy a new one. No more books... for now."

"A summer departure might be optimistic. Have you been working at Libros Revolución?"

"I have. I love that job, there's hardly any stress, and I get to look at books all day, scads of interesting stuff no one really wants. I'm practically vegetating, and the pay is more or less in line with the demands made on me."

"Do you take the 26 Short Line?"

"Almost every day, either to school or the bookstore. When Otis moves to the airport, I probably won't be able to teach there any longer."

"Do you ever see Otis students in Libros Revolución?"

"They wouldn't be caught dead in a communist bookstore."

I was tempted to ask Bernie about Temo, but I didn't want to get into a personal discussion on a pay phone. There was no telling where that conversation might lead. "I want to see you in person soon."

"We'll figure it out."

∞

The moment the library opened after the break, I went to the computer room to read my emails. There was one from Temo: "Great times on Tuesday. Tell me when you come to Los Angeles again. My new work schedule is Thursdays and Fridays."

I responded, "Will do," and added, "When can I sleep with you?" just to bother him. I knew he'd never sleep in the same bed with me as long as his parents lived in Los Angeles, but they would have to return to Mexico City eventually. I wondered if they bought or only rented their Regency style house above Sunset Plaza. Moira told me that it had once belonged to Paul Lynde, the flamboyant, wisecracking homosexual occupying the center square on *Hollywood Squares*, a television show that had been off the air for many years. Temo would have no idea who he was.

That afternoon, I saw Winston in the hallway and asked him about spring break. He said, "Big Sur was great. America is extraordinary, an immense landscape populated by little people."

Later, Carmen stopped by my studio and asked, "Do you want to come to Frances's tonight? We're going to watch a new show on TV."

I asked, "Which one?"

"*Buffy the Vampire Slayer*."

"Oh, I saw that movie. Is Paul Reubens in the TV version?"

She was tickled at the thought of Pee Wee Herman, Cal Arts' most famous disgraced alumnus, and said, "I don't think so, unless there's a scene that requires jerking off in a porno theater." She laughed as she shuffled a pile of papers and handed me a few stapled pages. "Try to read this script as soon as you can. We'll discuss it at dinner if you need to."

The script had my lines highlighted. I would play an interviewer in a scene shot in a video studio. I read my first line: "Clarice Lispector, where does this name, 'Lispector,' come from?"

The response: "I don't know. It's a Latin name, right? And I asked my father: since when had there been Lispectors in the Ukraine? And he said for generations and generations. I imagine the name rolled and rolled along, losing a few syllables, and transforming itself…." I wondered about the dialogue. Considering Carmen's other appropriations, I thought it unlikely that she wrote the text.

The show started at eight, and Carmen didn't want to miss a minute, so she planned an early dinner. At five o'clock, she rounded up Gregorio, Winston, and me. Frances was already at the apartment, where a pork loin was marinating in a batch of leftover sangria. At the market, we bought white wine and spinach for salad. I asked Carmen about the script. She said, "Amazing, isn't it? Clarice gave only one television interview during her life, and that's the transcript. She died a few months later."

"You'll do it verbatim, like *The Yellow Wallpaper*?"

She nodded and said, "We're going to reenact the footage as exactly as we can. We shoot day after tomorrow, after ten at night. Just show up in a long sleeve shirt, and someone will slick your hair back and put a beard on you. It'll be fun."

We entered a very smoky apartment. Frances looked concerned that something burning would ruin the flavor of her roast. She needn't have worried. The meal, a triumph of improvisation, succeeded brilliantly.

After we did the dishes, we all sat in the living room, and Gregorio made a point of sitting right next to me. Winston, who usually sat in the middle, was on the other side of Gregorio. Carmen and Frances somehow squeezed themselves into a large recliner. We settled in to watch two hours of television.

∞

Buffy the Vampire Slayer takes place mainly at Sunnydale High, a school in a small seaside city in California. Sunnydale is at a convergence of evil, mystical energies called the Hellmouth. This convinced me that the location must be Santa Barbara. Buffy, a popular girl from Los Angeles, moves to this provincial environment with her well-meaning but clueless mother, and tries to establish a social life and live down her reputation for antisocial violence, while passing her high school courses and driving stakes into the hearts of vampires. She finds a pair of delightfully wacky sidekicks in Xander and Willow, and a frenemy in mean girl Cordelia. An English librarian named Giles serves as Buffy's watcher and must train her in the ways of the Slayer, the chosen one, one girl in all the world who stands against the forces of darkness. The characters communicate in elaborate, witty banter that distracts spectators from the narrative's preposterous supernatural premise. Vampires, identifiable by deformed faces that make them look like psychotic pug dogs with fangs, live underground and travel in the sewers. When night falls, they roam around until Buffy kills them and they fall into piles of dust. One of the vampires, Angel, is not like the others. He has a pretty face and a soul, both of which enable him to have a love affair with Buffy, who at age sixteen is jailbait in the state of California.

During the first commercial break, Winston asked, "Is this what high school in America is like?"

Frances laughed and said, "I wish. Maybe in California."

I had always been slow to grasp a trend, and the case of *Buffy*'s cult was no exception. Carmen, Gregorio, and Winston had an immediate enthusiasm for the show—only Frances was openly skeptical—and while I didn't quite see its appeal, I kept my reservations to myself.

∞

On Wednesday, Carmen came by at a quarter to ten, and we went to a studio in a section of the building I had never seen, because it was reserved for film production classes. An assistant handed me a fake beard, and a few others moved some old furniture and a potted plant into the space. Carmen slipped into a dress and donned a wig styled in an unruly bob. She applied makeup and sat in her position to be lit. Someone guided me to a chair facing Carmen then rolled an AV cart into view so we could watch a VHS copy of the original we would be imitating. It was strictly for visual reference, as the dialogue was in Portuguese and there were no subtitles. I didn't think Carmen understood the language, but I wouldn't have put it past her. This woman seemed capable of anything.

We shot the video in sequences, none over seven minutes long, interrupted by slates bearing the logo of Brazil's state television network. Delivering our lines—Carmen's from cue cards and mine from index cards—was relatively easy. I asked my questions in an earnest monotone. Clarice/Carmen, in defiance of school policy, smoked as she spoke. During the interview, she fiddled constantly with a cellophane-wrapped pack, and never succeeded in removing the last cigarette. While distracted by this activity, she delivered a marvelous line: "The question of understanding isn't about intelligence, it's about feeling, about entering into contact."

At the very end of the interview, I asked, "Aren't you born again and refreshed with every new work?"

She responded, "We'll see if I can be born again. For now, I'm dead. I'm speaking from my tomb." After a few moments of silence, she said, "Cut," and just as quickly as it had been arranged, the set was broken down.

The video, called *Entrevista da Tumba* (Interview from the Tomb), took very little time to finish. The end credits were written in chalk on a slate and shot after my departure from the studio, and the editing was simplicity itself. I was slightly annoyed that Carmen got my name wrong, but then I thought that if the whole thing turned out to be an embarrassment, I could easily disassociate myself from it. In the end, the video was a resounding success, included in her thesis exhibition, and soon after, in various screenings of video art around the US. There was no explanation of the source material in the video itself, but instead, a synopsis (and the hearsay it generated) informed people of what they were watching. The piece found its place among a group of reenacted documentaries that garnered a lot of attention that year. I had also heard that Gus Van Sant would be directing a shot-by-shot remake of Alfred Hitchcock's *Psycho*. Something was "in the air," and Carmen's video was part of the trend. Whether this tendency, described as the apogee of postmodernism by its advocates, would last longer than a season or two, no one could predict.

∞

Around this time, we received our financial aid offers. Mine was more generous than I expected, while Gregorio got a disappointing scholarship, and Winston, who rarely deigned to speak in class and often left when he'd heard enough of what he considered nonsense, got almost none at all. Gregorio retreated to lick his wounds, but Winston exploded in anger. The fact that he had completed several accomplished paintings counted for nothing, he said, and I believed he was correct. His reputation suffered from the perception that our video was my work alone. Winston made a number of frantic long distance phone calls in languages I didn't understand, the result of which was his announcement that he would need to spend the summer in Europe.

Unbeknownst to all of us but Winston, Albania was in the midst of a crisis that threatened to become a civil war. I hadn't read anything about this, because in art school it was easy to miss major political events. I suggested that Winston make the faculty aware of what was going on in his country, and he said, "I have not seen Albania for many years. But yes."

"Have you heard from your family?" I asked.

He struggled to find words. "No. I have relatives in prison, waiting for trial. It is chaos there. I hope no one is executed."

I was at a total loss. I could only ask, "When do you leave?"

"As soon as I can. I go to Germany, then if it is safe, to Albania. It will be easier that way if I must leave quickly. Cities are being evacuated. I cannot say where my mother and sister are." He was in tears.

I hugged him and said, "Let me know if there's anything I can do."

"Tell the faculty they have wrecked me. Tell them about the civil war. I am sure they know nothing. Fuckers." He wiped his eyes. "I must arrange things in Germany. Perhaps some extra money can be found."

∞

Gregorio would also have to find a way to compensate for a financial shortfall. He said, "My sister will be in Santa Fe this summer working for the governor. She said I can share a house with her. I'll get a job somewhere."

I asked, "Will you give up the house in Saugus?"

"I don't think I'll have to. My roommates are staying here for the summer. They found jobs in the film industry."

"You'll spend the whole break in New Mexico?"

"Maybe. I can lend you my studio key so you can play records. Make sure they don't melt in the heat." He smiled weakly.

I was very disappointed. The three of us would be separated for months, and I would be stuck living in my studio without a car. I hugged Gregorio and said, "I'll miss you. Did you hear what happened to Winston?"

"He says he has to go to Europe. He didn't say why."

"Albania is a mess. His family is in danger. He's leaving soon."

Gregorio gave a serious nod and said, "So are Frances and Carmen. A friend of Frances's needs a roommate for a big apartment in Williamsburg, so she's off to New York. Carmen got a job at Video Data Bank, and she's moving to Chicago."

"I guess their relationship wasn't that serious." I paused for a moment. "Damn, I really will be all alone."

∞

In the weeks that remained to us as a group, watching *Buffy the Vampire Slayer* became a ritual for Frances, Carmen, Gregorio, Winston, and me. We started skipping our Monday classes and stumbling in on Tuesday afternoon after almost twenty-four hours of preparation, partying, and recovery. Since the Thursday night openings obliterated Friday classes, practically all that was left of our academic week was meetings on Wednesdays. Perhaps because I associated it with good times, I started to love *Buffy*, and hoped I could find a way to watch it in the absence of my friends.

In one of the last episodes we saw together, "The Pack," Buffy and her classmates take a field trip to the zoo, and near the hyena house, she sees what she takes to be two physically attractive heterosexual couples. They taunt her, but since she has sworn to attack only demons and they appear mortal, she does nothing. They move on to torment a nerd with a sketchbook, and the principal witnesses this, but the nerd covers for them. They take him to the hyena house, which is off limits. A zookeeper prevents Buffy and Willow from going after them and tells this story: "Hyenas are capable of understanding human speech. They follow humans around by day learning their names. At night, when the campfire dies, they call out to a person, and once they separate him, the pack devours him." Xander saves the nerd from being attacked, and the glowing eyes of the aggressors indicate that they have been possessed by a hyena's spirit. Xander later becomes enchanted, too. He helps the Pack bully weaklings, as they laugh loudly. After they devour a pig brought to campus as a school mascot, the principal attempts to punish the Pack, and for his trouble, he is killed and eaten.

Exhibiting brutal, animalistic behavior and conformist attitudes, the Pack represented the "cool kids" terrorizing high schools everywhere. Leaving aside the supernatural claptrap required by the plot, the episode was terrifying. At the end of it, Winston reiterated his question, "Is this what American high schools are like?"

Frances answered, "Yeah, exactly. Not the cannibalism part; not yet, anyway."

∞

The next day I saw Shelley, who ran the periodicals department, smoking just outside the door nearest the library. It was a mild infraction of the strict rules recently imposed on smokers at the school. She had always been kind to me, and I approved of her rebellion. I must have looked like a sad sack, because she asked me what was wrong. I mentioned that I'd be spending the summer in my studio. She said, "Do you need a job?"

I said, "That would be great."

"It's not much, sorting and filing periodicals, plus helping me decide which ones need to be deaccessioned, but it would give you access to the library."

I smiled. "That might be the only thing preventing me from going bonkers."

"I'm always happy to help preserve the mental health of our student body."

∞

In preparation for her departure, Frances packed up a van with her paintings and soon realized that a lot of her possessions wouldn't fit. Just before she left, she gave things away: art supplies to Gregorio, the large glass-topped table that she used as a palette to Winston, a boom box and collection of cassettes to me. I was the last person to see her on campus. She hugged me tightly and said, "Visit me once I get settled in New York."

"I'd love to. I've never even seen Brooklyn."

"Well then, you must."

One by one, I saw everyone I knew leave, until only Gregorio and I remained. When he packed his things and got on the freeway to points east, I cried.

∞

The summer was brutal in the Santa Clarita Valley, which was much hotter than my old neighborhood. The air conditioning in Cal Arts' main building ran during the day, but the Annex studios were never air conditioned during the summer. After five p. m., there was no ventilation anywhere. I would prop the doors open all night, when it got almost cool. I smelled sagebrush and hoped coyotes wouldn't wander inside. In a moment of desperation, I found a main power switch and flipped it so Winston's studio could have electricity. He had left his door unlocked for me, and I stayed inside with the air conditioner running on the days when I didn't have to work in the library.

My job was undemanding. I would usually finish by one p. m., but Shelley would allow me to stay until she left at four. Those extra hours would be spent reading periodicals, borrowing books from the stacks, or checking my email. I sent messages to Gregorio and Winston but didn't get responses from either of them for a while. I heard from Winston first. He was in Germany expecting to stay there the whole summer because the situation in Albania had deteriorated. I tried to get information in the library, but occasional news reports were all I could find. Albania was not a priority in international reporting, and the country's decades of isolation meant that any reporter entering the field had to cultivate contacts from scratch, an effort few were willing to undertake.

In its modern history, Albania was plagued by gangsters, some of them corrupted by the pursuit of power, others by the pursuit of money. Ramiz Alia, the successor of Enver Hoxha, was so bent on maintaining his grip on the country that he postponed any reforms that could have made the adoption of capitalism less brutal. With the International Monetary Fund calling the shots, this transition truly lived up to the term they used to describe the process, "shock therapy." Banking in the modern sense hardly existed in Albania, and people raised under socialism had little financial savvy when it came to applying for loans and finding places to put their money. Many of the ad hoc structures that developed in this void were in reality pyramid schemes, paying dividends to investors from a pool of money that grew only when new investors were found. Albania's economy showed little activity and produced nothing, while vast sums of money moved around, making it a perfect environment for organized crime. A network of pyramid schemes, unregulated and operating with the tacit approval of the government, collapsed completely in early 1997. This provoked widespread insurrection, during which thousands of people were killed, treasuries and arsenals were looted, and democratic governance, which had never been robust in the country, came to an end. In April, the United Nations launched Operation Alba to keep the peace, but money laundering and arms trafficking continued, and as of the summer of 1997, the country's future was uncertain. It was this Albania, engulfed in a social disaster, that Winston wisely decided to avoid during his summer vacation.

∞

I also emailed Temo, who always responded quickly. He was interested in meeting again, but under the circumstances, it wasn't feasible. I worked Monday, Wednesday and Friday, and the train didn't run on the weekends, so overnight trips to Los Angeles wouldn't work, even if Moira would lend him her apartment, which seemed unlikely. He asked about visiting me at my studio, but I was reluctant to say yes, because I thought he'd hate the heat and lack of amenities. He didn't offer to pay for a room, and I didn't ask. He probably wanted to avoid being seen as half of a male couple checking into a hotel together, even if everyone who saw us would be people we'd never meet again.

When it became clear that we couldn't see each other over the summer, Temo began sending me sex stories. They were relentlessly single-minded and almost infantile in their extremity, like an approximate translation of a manuscript by Sade.

I gave Temo prompts from time to time. When I asked him if he ever revealed his fantasies in confession, this inspired a torrent of filth about priests. I got very aroused when I read his messages. I began to print them out and save them for later so I could masturbate to them in private. I hardly contributed a word to the correspondence, yet the flow of emails continued. How much of what he wrote was fantasy and how much was fact I couldn't say, but something from his past must have inspired him. He recounted an episode about cruising the public toilets at the Basilica of Our Lady of Guadalupe, where he had bought the necklace he never took off. That story had a ring of truth to it, and I thought I could encourage him to reveal more about his actual experiences. He began to tell me about a powerful priest named Marcial Maciel and his group Regnum Christi, which had a youth outreach program that amounted to a fascist army of beautiful young men and boys devoted absolutely to Jesus, and to their leader. I supposed that he had been a member of this organization when he was young, but there was no way of confirming it.

∞

I had a break from Temo's messages when Gregorio sent me a one line email with his phone number. I called him that evening. His sister answered. She shouted, "Goyo!" and he picked up the receiver after a minute.

"How are you?" I asked.

"Oh, fine. I'm working in an art gallery. It's really silly, but I have a little money."

"When are you returning?"

He said, "August. I'm sick of Santa Fe, and I want to get back to California."

I told him, "I'm so bored. It's scary here during the summer. And incredibly hot."

"How are my records?"

"Um, they haven't melted yet. I open your studio door at night to let the place cool down."

"They turned off the air conditioning?"

"Yeah, only Winston's studio has AC these days. I stay in there on my days off. By the way, I miss you."

There was a pause, during which I sensed Gregorio's discomfort with talking on the phone. He finally said, "Thanks."

"Well, I should get going. This call is costing a fortune."

"Have you heard from Winston?" he asked before I hung up.

"Only a couple of short emails. The situation in Albania is shit, so he's staying in Germany. Have you heard from him?"

"He called me here once, but I was at work, so he left a message." Gregorio lowered his voice. "It was really embarrassing. But you know Winston, he doesn't care. My sister listened to it before I did. God, what a mess."

I tried to stifle a laugh. "His shamelessness is his best feature. I suppose your sister has no idea who you're involved with."

Gregorio warmed up. "Oh, she has an idea now." There was another pause. "I should go. Nice to hear your voice."

I said, "I'll try to call again. I promise I won't leave any compromising messages."

FOURTEEN

A few days later, I called Moira, and she answered breathlessly. "I just got in. How are you?"

"Oh, you know, losing my mind in Santa Clarita."

"Do you want to go out and do something?"

"I won't ask you to drive sixty miles on my account."

"Are you alone up there?"

"Yes. My best friends have fled for the summer... or graduated."

"As soon as I take a shower, I'm coming to get you."

"Okay, if you're not too tired."

"I sit behind a desk all day. I'm happy to do it. Pack a bag. You can spend the weekend here."

"Thanks. You're a life saver."

Moira picked me up at the school's front entrance in Temo's Miata. I gave her a surprised look, and she explained, "He's in Mexico City for a while, and he told me he'd buy a new car when he got back into town. Pretty extravagant." As we merged onto the freeway, Moira asked me, "How long have you two been having an affair?"

I stammered and blushed. "Um, I wouldn't call it an affair."

"I'm not angry, I just wondered why neither of you saw fit to tell me."

There was an interval of silence while Moira waited for an explanation. I said, "So I have had sex with Temo, but he specifically told me to keep that secret from you. We're *not* boyfriends. Obviously. He gave his car to you, not me."

Moira said, "You would have totaled it anyway."

"Fair enough. I don't have much luck with cars." I asked, "How did you find out about us?"

"One day at work, I saw an email he was writing about some crazy sexual fantasies. Or at least I think they were fantasies."

"He's quite the pornographer."

"I asked him about it, and he started telling me about a double life: dinners with the parents, me as his beard, pursuing a PhD at UCLA on one hand, and an incredibly depraved sex life with various men on the other."

I blushed again. "How much did he tell you?"

"Enough that I won't lecture you about safer sex."

"I don't know anything about the other men, but I have no trouble believing he's been around the block. Makes me feel really special," I said sarcastically.

Moira changed the subject and asked, "Did he talk to you about his religious upbringing?"

"I wondered if the stories about priests in his emails were true. He mentioned something called Regnum Christi, but it seemed too weird to be credible. I don't remember all the details. Sorry, not Catholic."

Moira gave me a summary: "Regnum Christi is an ultraconservative Mexican lay organization associated with the Legion of Christ. It was founded by Marcial Maciel, who is without doubt one of the most evil men in the modern Catholic Church, and that's really saying something. He's insanely anticommunist, but I don't know if this is sincere or merely a way of kissing John Paul II's ass.

Maciel's special relationship with the Pope has allowed him to behave with no limits whatsoever, molesting hundreds of boys, and living secretly with women who bore him sons, whom he also molested. His crimes have been covered up with official silence. The Pope admires his genius for raising money—billions of dollars, which funded clandestine political activities in Eastern Europe, as well as houses and sports cars and trips abroad for Maciel. The highest officials in Rome do nothing, even though serious complaints have been lodged by his victims. He surrounds himself with clever boys and athletes, no cripples and no one who looks too indigenous, only 'white' Mexicans. Temo was probably one of them."

"Holy shit."

"No kidding."

"Do you know anything else about his past?"

"He went to UNAM in Mexico City and University of Chicago, but that didn't turn out so well."

I asked, "What did he do at U of C?"

Moira took a breath and started another story. "Temo studied with Allan Bloom, whom you may know as the author of the book *The Closing of the American Mind*. Bloom called himself a philosopher, and he got quite a few people to believe him. I think he was a complete fraud, wielding charismatic authority rather than arguments, and impressing his students with wild, campy *ex cathedra* pronouncements. Following Plato, whose writings he claimed to know, he believed in pedagogical Eros. That was his justification for sexually harassing and exploiting every handsome young man who crossed his path. But he didn't always get lucky. He often criticized the younger generation for being unerotic and incapable of appreciating the values of 'friendship' when they resisted his advances. Anyway, that troll took a liking to our Temo, who had a history with pervy old authoritarians, possibly starting with his own father." Moira paused. "Temo told me that he was close to

Bloom while he was dying of AIDS, and—this is incredible—jerked him off on his death bed."

I couldn't help but laugh at that last part, as pathetic as it was. I said, "Now I've heard everything."

She finished, "After Bloom's death, his boyfriend's hatred of Temo became so poisonous that he withdrew from school and moved across the United States."

It occurred to me that I might have heard about Temo from someone else. I couldn't believe it was just a coincidence, so I dug the address book out of my bag and looked up my friend Raúl, the man who taught me everything I knew about fist fucking. He had received his PhD from the University of Chicago, and his time there might have overlapped with Temo's.

As soon as we arrived at Moira's apartment, I called Raúl and asked him about the *fresa* he had known some years before, a man he had fisted, but from whom he parted on less than friendly terms. When I asked his name, Raúl said, "Cuauhtémoc. I called him Temo."

I exclaimed, "I know him!"

Raúl asked, "Did you fist him?"

"What do you think? Hey, do you mind if I put you on speaker phone? I have a friend here who works with him."

"Sure."

"Moira, tell Raúl what Temo does now."

"He works at a radical bookstore in Los Angeles called Libros Revolución."

"Holy shit," said Raúl.

I let out a chuckle. "That's what I said."

Raúl warned, "The guy was a reactionary when I knew him. He was praising Augusto Pinochet and Francisco Franco. I couldn't hear about it anymore. I didn't want to be involved in his fantasy of getting fisted by some big fascist daddy. That pissed him off. We stopped seeing each other. I bet he works for the CIA. It was his goal."

"What?!" Moira exclaimed.

There followed a long and involved conversation in which the three of us talked about our experiences with Temo. We collated the stories in an attempt to construct a plausible biography. The crux of the matter was what happened in Chicago. In one version, Temo became disgusted by the cult of Allan Bloom and the excesses of personal behavior it encouraged, and saw a connection to what he'd experienced in Mexico at the hands of Marcial Maciel and his followers; he had a change of heart, came to Los Angeles and started working at Libros Revolución out of a sincere wish to think and act in another way; his life was not entirely free, because he was still tied down by obligations to his parents, who held a family inheritance over his head. In the other version, Temo, unable to handle the pressure of graduate school after the death of his advisor and in need of an alternative career, was recruited by the CIA, which gave him an assignment to observe and report on activists in Los Angeles while working at a leftist bookstore and posing as a PhD student at UCLA; politically, he was still his parents' son, but he couldn't deny the desires that compelled him to seek out the sexual scenes in which Raúl and I, as well as many other men, had taken part.

∞

That evening, Moira and I met Bernie for dinner. He was in fine form. Since Moira now knew as much as I did about Temo, he was no longer off limits as a topic of conversation. We told Bernie about what we had learned in the last few hours, and he sat there listening to us with a look of wonder on his face. After we had finished, Bernie said, "That guy reminds me of some of the students at ICP, very privileged Europeans who went into photojournalism. The profession was all about consuming exotic disasters—poverty in India or Africa. It was also less demanding then. With the recession, it's shrunk considerably and now involves more warfare, because of the incessant disaster in the Balkans. No longer so attractive to rich dilettantes. Maybe they work for the CIA now."

Moira rolled her eyes and asked him, "Did you know about his sex life?"

Bernie shifted his weight uncomfortably and responded, "He seemed pretty repressed and tormented. But once I overheard him talking on the phone. I assume the person on the other end of the line was an older man. He kept talking about his 'pussy.' It was so monomaniacal that it sounded like a parody. I had to restrain myself from laughing. I thought maybe he did phone sex as a job, but then why would someone of his class bother with such demanding work? One day I arrived a little early, and I saw him in the middle of something heavy, probably with the man he had been speaking to on the phone. I shut the door to the back room almost immediately, but in one second, I got an eyeful. I don't think he noticed me… too high on poppers, and who knows what else." Bernie had been focusing on some faraway spot during the story, then suddenly, he looked at us as though he had snapped out of a trance.

As I looked down at my half-eaten dinner, I said, "Well, thanks for that." I felt an irrepressible jealousy. I never once considered monogamy as a possibility, but in vulnerable moments, I allowed myself to think that Temo and I were in some sort of a relationship. I wondered how many others had been lulled into the same complacent dream.

I looked up and noticed that Moira was at a loss. She said, "I should be getting you back to campus before it gets too late."

"That's a good idea." I was happy that my own interactions with Temo had not been subjected to scrutiny and wanted to leave before the conversation took an embarrassing turn.

Bernie wrote down his email address and said, "Here, I keep forgetting to give you this. Now you don't have to call me from a pay phone when you want to communicate."

"Great, thanks." I took the slip of paper and put it in my bag.

Not long after our dinner, the sex messages I was receiving from Temo came to an end. A few weeks later, Moira and I got an email announcing Temo's marriage to Julieta, a friend from his undergraduate days. We asked ourselves if we had ever really known this man who left our lives just as mysteriously as he had come into them. We both felt numb.

∞

Back in my studio, the marathon of summer heat and boredom continued, with only my job as a relief from the torment. One of my duties was processing periodicals. As soon as they arrived in the department, I would mark them with a stamp reading "California Institute of the Arts Library," enter the name and issue number into a database, and place them on a cart for shelving later. Occasionally, I saw a magazine that intrigued me, and since the pace of summer work was slow, I would read it before I processed it. When the library received the July 1997 issue of *SPIN*, I was interested enough to take it to my studio.

The article "Too Cool for School" by Dennis Cooper presented young artists and their work in the context of a mass market music magazine. Up until that time, journalists generally relied on a small repertoire of well-worn stereotypes in portraying artists: the antisocial freak, the respected visionary, and more recently, the confidence man capable of turning nothing (the worthless raw materials of art, studios in slum neighborhoods) into something (valuable commodities and renovated buildings). "Too Cool for School" told a story of art as lifestyle, focusing on a group of students at UCLA talking, partying, and above all, making lots of things. They seemed poised to have careers as impressive as their famous instructors—Chris Burden, Paul McCarthy, and Charles Ray. The article reinforced two notions that gained currency since the exhibition *Helter Skelter*: that Los Angeles was a place apart from (and to a large extent indifferent to) what was happening in New York, yet still taken seriously in the art world; and that MFA graduates could make reasonably secure bourgeois livings for themselves on the proceeds of an art practice, as long as they attended the most selective schools and made the right connections.

∞

Gregorio returned to town in August. When he arrived on campus, he found me in the studio in my underwear, listening to "The Queen Is Dead" blasting from his stereo across the hall. The week before, Cal Arts security had finally discovered Winston's door open and locked me out. I was stuck with nothing but a fan blowing hot air to cool me off. I must have looked pretty wretched. As we hugged, I said, "I'm starving. Let's go to Saugus Café."

Over the meal, we discussed our summers. He told me that Santa Fe was a sinister place, full of people with little to do but buy Indian artifacts and decorate their houses during "the season," by which he thought they meant the opera season, but he wasn't sure. Most of the state of New Mexico was poor, and these idle rich folks stuck out among a population that had been there for centuries. I asked him how it was to live with his sister as an adult, and he said, "Not bad. She's ambitious. I don't want to do anything that would ruin her political career."

"So no orgies at Goyo's place in Santa Fe?"

Gregorio looked over his shoulder and said, "Of course not. I'm glad to be in California. I left early." He paused and played with his plate of eggs. "Have you heard from Winston?"

"Not much. I guess you know as much as I do."

After our meal, Gregorio invited me to his house. I wasn't sure what his intentions were. Finally, he said, "You can sleep here."

We made some fumbling attempts at having sex, but it soon became clear that we weren't very compatible in that way, or that Winston's presence was too sorely missed for us to have any fun without him. Still, it felt good to have companionship and affection after all those weeks of loneliness and discomfort in my studio.

For the rest of the month, we continued to sleep together at night. During the day, Gregorio listened to music and sweated profusely while trying to get some painting done in his studio. When I didn't have to work, we would go on trips, our favorite destination being Ventura, with its beach and great thrift stores. The end of Route 126 was planted with laurel bushes, and whenever we saw their bright flowers, we cheered. It was always cooler along the coast, so we spent whole days there, eating burritos at Corrales, shopping for records at Wild Planet, and looking for bargains. In the thrift stores of Oxnard and Santa Paula, people would speak to Gregorio in Spanish, because he was dark-skinned, but he would always answer in English, even though he knew Spanish rather well. One day, he found a pristine UK copy of *Strangeways, Here We Come* at the Retarded Citizens Thrift Store in downtown Ventura, near the mission. He was overjoyed at what seemed to be nothing short of a miracle. He decided then and there to extend the time period of his collection to the end of September 1987, when *Strangeways* was first released. On our way back to Santa Clarita, I asked a question I had thought about for some time, "Why do you like English pop music so much?"

Gregorio exhaled loudly. "You mean, because I'm Hispanic? Nobody would ask that if you collected records by The Smiths."

"Yeah, I guess that's what I meant. And you're right, no one questions me when I play one of your records."

He explained, "I have no connection to Mexican pop music. Spanish isn't my native language. My parents speak Spanish, but they don't listen to Mexican music or watch *Siempre en Domingo*, either. They associate that stuff with their parents. My generation speaks English, but at the same time, we feel alienated from the mainstream white culture of the United States. We try to occupy a neutral territory. So we have two main choices: black music from America, or English pop music. I have cousins who listen hip hop and Prince and R & B oldies. I don't really care for that stuff myself, but I understand why they like it." He looked over at me, and noticing I wasn't satisfied with his explanation, tried another approach. "Listen, if you're disgusted by Mexican *machismo* and you see a picture of Robert Smith with all that teased hair and makeup, it has a huge impact. You know, English pop music has a great tradition of androgyny and ridiculing middle class morality."

I said, "There's a sense of celebration wrapped up in resentment… and masochism."

"I'm not sure if I should kiss you or slap your face."

I responded, "As a tattoo artist once said, 'Laugh now, cry later.'"

FIFTEEN

When fall registration began, Winston hadn't shown up on campus yet. In a panic, Gregorio and I went through the motions and hoped for the best. During the second week of the semester, at the last possible moment, Winston arrived at LAX and called from a pay phone to ask Gregorio to pick him up. We went together and found Winston bedraggled and exhausted in the international terminal. Traffic on the 405 was nightmarish, and it took us over an hour to get to campus. We were squeezed into Gregorio's truck the whole time, and I regretted coming along. I apologized to Winston, and he dismissed it. "I wanted to see you," he said with real affection. Gregorio dropped me off at my studio, then took Winston back to his house in Saugus.

∞

The mood of our second year was completely different from the first. Now that we knew our way around, there was little left to discover, aside from what the incoming students were like. From the outset, the most vocal faction of them took every opportunity to belittle the institution, the faculty, and the second year students. They were expansive on the subject of what they found objectionable, but when asked what they really cared about, they went mute. Their criticisms amounted to consumerist complaints about a product (an art school education) that they thought wasn't worth the amount of money they—or more likely their parents—were paying for it. Predictably, the only topic that engaged them was shopping.

The shopping artists formed a clique centered around a guy named Brad. He came from Atlanta, where he ran a small arts venue, and he had a talent for attracting followers. He freely expressed his disdain for anyone who didn't belong to his circle. The group respected only fame and beauty, or at least what appeared famous and beautiful by their lights. They quickly developed a vocabulary impenetrable to outsiders and often told inside jokes that sounded devastating to them. Any student who didn't live up to a standard of "cool" that was never explicitly defined became a target of ridicule. The clique usually appeared in pairs or trios. They instinctively understood that their tactics only worked if they ganged up on people.

Everyone in the clique was pretty, especially the men, and that led me to suspect that Brad was a closet case and took his sexual frustration out on weaklings—called "uglos" in the group's parlance— who could be easily terrorized. The first year master's students had all read "Too Cool for School" and had conceived the idea that one day they would be art stars. They counted on a beguiling pose and a clever line of patter to get them to the top of the art world. They probably rehearsed what they would say and how they would dress if *SPIN* magazine interviewed them. They barely attended to the production of objects, not because they considered themselves to be conceptual artists, but because they had little patience for hard work.

I gave this gang of bullies a nickname taken from an episode of *Buffy the Vampire Slayer*: the Pack. Gregorio picked up on it, and soon several of us had our own inside jokes about these vacant, brutal hyenas in designer clothes. The Pack poisoned the atmosphere, and most of the second year MFA students decided to concentrate on their own work rather than risk being drawn into the foul new social dynamic in the Art School.

∞

The highlight of the fall semester was an interesting roster of visiting artists, including Jack Goldstein, who was returning to the alma mater he had left about twenty-five years before. The films he showed were visually stunning, staging concise conceptual jokes in evocative images. Goldstein himself seemed the worse for wear. He was openly resistant to giving an artist's talk, and spoke with bitterness about his career. As far as he was concerned, everyone who was anyone had screwed him over.

When the lecture ended, I saw Paul making his way to the door. I got out of my seat and followed him. "Hey, what are you doing here?"

Paul turned around with a start and said, "Well darling, you're a sight for sore eyes. I came to check out the new talent, and what should I see but a poster for the Jack Goldstein medicine show?"

We went to the student lounge, where he held court on the subject of our visiting artist. Gregorio and Winston joined us. I asked, "Do you know Goldstein?"

"I have known him, in the biblical sense, one could say."

We were all nonplussed, and Gregorio said, "He's not gay."

"No," Paul replied, "but a drug addict will do anything for a fix, and some of the less scrupulous elements of society have been known to take advantage."

"You are a legendary whore," I said with grudging admiration.

Paul shrugged and said, "No, whores get paid." He raised his voice. "Gather 'round, children, and I'll tell you the cautionary tale of the great Goldstein." He cleared his throat and asked, "Did you know he was also a painter?" We all shook our heads. "In the postmodern sense, dearies. He used to refer to the assistants who produced his paintings by the demeaning term 'tapers,' because their work consisted of masking off with tape the parts of the canvas to be filled in with acrylics, like paint-by-numbers on a grand scale. Goldstein chose the source images and color schemes, and with stunning cynicism, left the rest to his assistants."

"They are terrible paintings," Winston said with confidence.

"You'd be surprised, my young friend. They looked ever so dolly in four-color repro. A masterpiece in every magazine. The market was sadly indifferent to those films and performances he talked about tonight. The way he really accumulated the fortune that went up his nose was by painting. Goldstein made his climb with the help of women he used like Kleenex. He fucked them, then abandoned each one when someone more powerful or solicitous came along. He had his whole strategy laid out, but he didn't understand the problem of the 'mid-career artist.' The art world loves hot young things and decrepit old survivors. In between, an artist can't get arrested."

"What do you mean?" asked Gregorio.

"A colloquial expression from the business of show, my dear. The vast desert of middle age, when most artists disappear into academia, has swallowed many a career. But the great Goldstein simply couldn't cope. He was the classic '80s cocaine addict, *folie des grandeurs* for days until he had to get some sleep at night. And that's when he started taking heroin. Once he made a few baby steps down Smack Alley, it was the beginning of the end. Soon his reputation and his bank balance were practically nil. The stories of his dissolution are legion. In an effort to raise cash, he tried to sell the same painting under the table to three different collectors. That's not the sort of thing a dealer will put up with, as you can imagine. After burning his bridges in New York, he worked his way west—first stop, Chicago, then finally the poor junky landed on the West Coast, San Bernardino to be exact, where his long-suffering Cockney parents owned an abode of some description."

"I thought he was Canadian," I said, dimly remembering the artist's bio from a press release.

Paul continued, "His mater and pater are East London Jews who immigrated to Montreal. Of course, when the 'good son' made a killing in the art racket, they decamped to sunnier climes. Unfortunately, they were not set for life. Soon Jack was soaking *them* for moolah, rather than the other way around. Poor Ma Goldstein had to take in sewing to make ends meet. But as much of a bastard as old Jack could be, people still loved him. Friends who knew him in his prime would ask, 'Where's Jack?' of any poor sap they thought might be sympathetic to their cause. If there was even a whiff of a clue, they would follow it up with the query, 'Is he fat or skinny?' The former meant that he was off drugs; the latter meant that he was using again.

"The great Goldstein spent his strangest period in East Los Angeles, in an RV without plumbing, surrounded by wild dogs and delicious gangbangers. I met him at that dire moment. It was long before your mother found religion, mind you, and I was still dealing illegal substances to make a living. Suffice it to say that that cul-de-sac next to the freeway was the scariest place I'd ever seen, and I've had a gander at Nancy Reagan's twat. He's just a shadow of the man he once was. So bitter."

∞

I had signed up for a meeting with Goldstein, and the next day, he came to my studio about twenty minutes late. I decided to see him first thing in the morning. I guessed that whatever demons had driven him to his current state of ruin were more likely to descend as the day wore on. He looked at the bare walls of my studio and immediately said, "You're not making any work. Why am I here?" I directed his attention to a small combination VCR and television, where I had cued up the video I made with Winston, *American Dream*. He sat through it without complaint, then asked me, "Did you write that crap?"

"It was a collaboration with a friend."

"Did you shoot it?"

"Yes."

He harrumphed. "That's the best part. This town has turned into something horrible, and it's good you're showing it. So what do you want to do, become an irrelevant experimental filmmaker?"

"I'm not sure. Are all experimental filmmakers irrelevant?"

"Yeah, it's been that way since the '70s. Don't they teach you that here?"

"I can't say they've gotten the bad news."

Goldstein turned and faced me to emphasize his point: "The market is the only thing that matters in the art world, and the only thing that matters in the art market is painting. Don't let anyone tell you differently."

"But I don't know how to paint."

He became adamant. "I'm a filmmaker and writer, and I did performances. I don't know how to paint, either. I made paintings anyway, and it worked, too... until it didn't."

I looked at his mouth as he said this. He had only a few teeth left, and all of them were discolored. I could tell he was handsome once, but had stopped caring about his appearance long ago. I had heard about junkies' aversion to water, and I doubted that he had bathed before coming to school. As this occurred to me, he gave me a sidelong glance as though he knew what I was thinking. I asked, "Is being a painter the only way to be an artist?"

"It's the only way to be the best. And if you don't aim for the top, why bother? The only real artists are the ones who can support themselves from their practice. These clowns who get teaching jobs in Illinois or somewhere are just posers. They don't really know what's going on. You have to develop a signature style distinct from everyone else, and that's not easy. Then you have to exploit it with the help of galleries that are at the same time exploiting you. The only way to make it work is to sell paintings for so much money that you can live well and say 'fuck you' to everyone. Anything else is just a hobby."

"I think your films are fantastic."

He snapped, "Who the fuck can see them? They're for a tiny audience, and I never made a cent from them."

When he calmed down, I asked him, "What do you suggest I do?"

He looked me in the eye once more and said, "Move to New York the minute you get out of school. It's the only place to live if you want to be taken seriously as an artist. Don't hold back. You have to go at it full force and do whatever it takes to realize your ambitions. You have ambitions, don't you?" I nodded. "Then if you want something, go get it. And remember there are a few hundred other assholes who want the same thing." He looked at his watch. He had spent only twenty-five minutes with me, but he was ready to go. "Can you take me to my next meeting?"

"Sure. Thanks for your time."

As we walked to the studio of the person who was next on the list, he said, "Don't make the same mistakes I did. Everyone in the art world is a fucking monster, but I can't blame them for my problems. I did this to myself. Drugs help for a while, but they catch up with you in the end. Look at me. I was on heroin. Now I'm on methadone. Methadone is awful." Goldstein knocked on the student's door, but there was no answer. We waited in uncomfortable silence as he grumbled and fidgeted. Then with an utterly bereft look in his eye he said his parting words, "I sacrificed everything to be a famous artist. I stepped on anyone who stood in my way. I wrecked every relationship I ever had. It wasn't worth it."

∞

I heard from the visiting artist coordinator that Dennis Cooper was coming to campus for studio visits, and I asked to be informed when the sign-up sheet would be posted. The following Monday morning, Gregorio, Winston, and I went to the Art School office and reserved meetings. Dennis's time was limited, and after we were done, there were only three time slots left, all of which were taken by lunchtime. Members of the Pack, who undoubtedly would have wanted meetings with him, missed out entirely. They said they were "going to Las Vegas" that weekend, but I had seen them around campus. I later learned that this was their expression for doing drugs. They were sleeping off a cocaine binge while the rest of us signed up for meetings. When word of this reached them, Brad flew into a rage, but hid his anger, and in his most charming manner, attempted to convince the visiting artist coordinator, the administrative assistant, and any faculty members who would listen that an injustice had been done, and another sign-up sheet needed to be posted at a more reasonable hour. No one yielded to his pleas, so a list of scrawled names appeared in the space beneath Dennis's last appointment. It was extremely unlikely that he'd want to stay on campus until ten p. m., but as far as the disappointed were concerned, this last ditch effort was worth a try.

The Pack worshiped Dennis Cooper, due partly to his reputation as an author of "transgressive fiction"—I doubt they had read it, but they had certainly heard about it—and partly to his cultural journalism, especially "Too Cool for School." This article, plus his occasional reviews, gave them the impression that he was an important arbiter who had the ability to "write about the art of tomorrow today," as one of his colleagues at *Artforum* put it. I had actually read his fiction, and I thought he would have useful things to say, if not to me, then to Winston or Gregorio.

I showed Dennis *American Dream*, and he appreciated the shots of the "master planned community" of Santa Clarita being built. He had grown up in the San Gabriel Valley, and he spoke with genuine affection about the region. Without revealing who had told me, I mentioned that someone advised me to move to New York after graduation. I said that this seemed like a good idea, because I might get more attention for my work there.

"You shouldn't do it," he said. "Don't get me wrong, New York is great. It's the center of American culture, but that's its problem. Thousands of people there are devoted to finding the latest art, writing about it, bringing it to a wider audience, and once they're finished, dropping it and moving on. If they 'discover' you, you'll get pigeonholed right away as the guy who does this one very special thing. Maybe there'll be others who do something similar, and you'll get lumped in with them. They'll call you a group or a generation, and there's no escaping that. After a few years, you and your friends will get a footnote in the history books if you're lucky. Then it'll be over. The Sex Pistols did it all in eighteen months, but what artist or writer can?"

I asked, "What happens if I stay here?"

"People tend to curate artists into group shows if they know them from the scene, but then, if you're on the scene too long, they get sick of you. If you're an LA artist, no one in New York will have a chance to get bored with your work. New Yorkers won't have a context for what you do, so they'll dismiss it as folk art or something. In the short run, that'll be frustrating, but if you're persistent and follow your instincts, you won't ever go away. You'll be out here all along making work in your own way without anyone looking over your shoulder. New York will catch up with you eventually, and by the time that happens, you'll be a mature artist. You'll probably never be part of mainstream art history, but your career will last twenty or thirty years longer."

I didn't respond immediately, because it took me a while to absorb everything Dennis had said. As I thought about it after he left, I realized that he had given me the best advice about art I had ever received.

SIXTEEN

Gregorio, Winston, and I decided to celebrate the end of fall semester with a trip to one of my favorite bars, HMS Bounty. I invited Moira and Bernie to join us. Gregorio was the designated driver by default, and I offered to take us home if he drank too much. His truck was uncomfortable, as usual. I had forgotten how difficult it was to park in Koreatown, and I really wanted to get out as he went round and round the block. Just as we were about to give up and go somewhere else, a space opened up only a short walk from the bar.

Moira was already there and had saved a booth for us. She was drinking a Shirley Temple, so I understood that she had driven. I decided to order the same, while Gregorio and Winston drank hard liquor. Moira passed me a key to her apartment across the table and said, "You can stay at my place over Christmas again if you need to."

"Thanks so much. I was going to ask…"

"It's fine, just water the plants, please."

I said, "I'll be out of town for part of the time, only a few days. I have to see my mother for Christmas."

"Good for you. How is she doing?"

"I'm going to find out. I rarely call her. I'm a bad son. In my defense, it's tough to stay in touch when you don't have a phone line."

Everyone around the table looked a bit glum when I said this, as we all had troubled relationships with family. To break the mood, Gregorio announced that he'd be bringing Winston home for the holidays again, but this time, he'd tell his parents about their relationship. Winston, who was unaware that his lover's hometown was named after an American game show, raised his glass and shouted, "To Truth and Consequences!"

We talked with Moira about what was going on at Cal Arts, and she said, "I think it's gotten a lot more conservative." She turned to me. "I bet you haven't made any porn, either."

I shook my head. "There's still time. And besides, I had a proposition recently." Gregorio and Winston perked up at the mention of my sex life. I said to them, "Nothing happened, so you can settle down."

They both looked disappointed. Gregorio asked, "Who came on to you?"

Bernie suddenly showed up, about an hour late, which said something about the availability of buses in Los Angeles at night. He apologized and sat down with a drink in his hand. He asked, "What were you talking about?"

Winston responded, "Sex, of course."

I provided some background information for Moira and Bernie, "The first year MFAS are a bunch of little bitches, all attitude and no ideas. One of the guys who goes along with the popular crowd doesn't seem to fit in. I've noticed him letting his guard down and doing things like telling the truth and having emotions. And he isn't bad looking. His name is Jerry."

Gregorio asked, "Isn't he straight?"

Bernie replied, "So is spaghetti until you heat it up."

We all laughed, and I continued, "A couple of nights ago, Jerry, who was very drunk and horny, barged into my studio with a hard-on sticking out of his pants and asked for a blowjob. I sent him away."

Winston said, "Life is better without a gag reflex."

I said, "I'm not going to blow him. He seems like a pretty good guy, despite his unsavory associations, but I don't want those people knowing anything about me."

"The sluttiest guy in the Art School has acquired scruples all of a sudden." Gregorio's remark came across as nastier than he intended, and he immediately followed it up with, "I'm sorry."

"Well, if I could convince him to strip and jerk off for me, I'd be happy to document it. Then I could make some porn. Who knows what I'll do for a living when I get out of school? I should start practicing now."

Moira said, "Speaking of your future, I'm giving up my apartment in the spring. Do you want it when you graduate?"

Without a moment's hesitation, I said, "Yes, please."

"The neighborhood is getting more convenient all the time. The subway will be extended to Hollywood, and North Hollywood after that. There'll be a station at Vermont and Beverly."

"That's great. What will you be doing?" I asked.

Moira thought for a moment and said, "I'm not sure yet. I may get a PhD."

"Oh, I hope not like Temo got a PhD," I said with air quotes.

I was smiling, but Moira wasn't. "That guy." She blushed a deep shade of red. "Because of him, the government probably has a file on me."

"Do you know anything more?" I asked.

"Nothing, but he'd be delighted that we're talking about him. I keep turning it over in my mind, and I still can't figure out who he really was. He paid lip service to leftist politics when he worked with me, but he never expressed a single original thought of his own."

Winston abruptly interjected, "That is an advantage for a communist functionary."

Gregorio said, "I bet he's inside so many closets that he doesn't know what to think. He reminds me a little bit of my father. He has an ideal of who he should be, but he can't live up to it, ever. So he takes it out on his only son. With love, of course."

At that moment, Paul, whom I hadn't seen in months, came up to us and asked, "Mind if I join you?" Before any of us could say a word, he squeezed himself into a narrow gap next to me. "Much obliged, dearies. There's a foul miscreant I'm trying to avoid at present."

"Only one?" I asked.

"To my certain knowledge, yes." His face brightened and he said, "You haven't introduced me to your friends." He turned to Moira and Bernie and extended his hand. "I'm Paul, like the great villain of the New Testament."

Bernie laughed and said, "Your reputation precedes you."

"Thank you," he said with the solemnity of a church lady.

I asked, "What have you been up to?"

"I've just returned from a trip up north. I was at the gracious home of New Narrative author and impeccable clone Bob Glück for the wake of Miss Kathy Acker."

I exclaimed, "I had no idea she died!"

"Darling, under what rock have you been living? She had been ill with breast cancer for over a year." He picked up my drink accidentally, and when he tasted something non-alcoholic, he grimaced. "The poor thing got a double mastectomy, then turned her back on Western medicine."

Moira said, "That couldn't have gone well."

Paul continued, "Get this. She fell to the clutches of some outrageous charlatans: an astrologer she consulted every half hour on all matters, including her bowel movements; a creature called a past life regressionist; and worst of all, a bunch of so-called healers who assured her she was cancer-free, when actually her whole body was riddled with it. I hope they get sued into a parallel dimension, the cunts." He looked at Moira. "Pardon my French."

Moira said, "Don't worry, I've heard everything. She must have been in tremendous pain."

Paul nodded. "Acker wasted away to nothing, and when she was too far gone for a hospital to help her, she was spirited over the border to a facility for hopeless cases. She died last month at a Tijuana alternative medicine clinic, in Room 101." He took a sip of his own drink. "When he found out, Alan Moore said, 'There's nothing that woman can't turn into a literary reference.'"

I laughed but Winston remained silent. I turned to him and explained, "Room 101 is the torture chamber in *1984*." He nodded tentatively. I asked, "Have you read Orwell, Winston Smith?"

"Not yet."

"You really are the perfect Cal Arts student, naming yourself after the protagonist of a novel you've never read." I turned to Paul and asked, "Now that her idol is dead, will Carmen keep up her Acker imitation?"

Paul answered, "I heard from Frances that Chicago didn't work out for Carmen. She's back in New York, living with her parents."

I said to Bernie, "I thought *you'd* be back in New York by now."

"That was the plan, but I'm still saving up money. I may need to buy a new car. That Ford is a total lemon." He raised his glass and said with a crooked grin, "Buy American." He turned serious and fretted, "I shouldn't have brought my book collection with me. Otherwise, I could just fly. I don't know." The difficult topic and all the drinking had left him confused. He whined, "I think I'm stuck in Los Angeles."

"Join the club," I said. "I have flight fantasies all the time, but then I ask, 'Where the hell would I go?' I've never been able answer that question. At least I hate this city less than other places I've been."

Moira laughed and said, "Spoken like a true Angeleno."

After a couple more drinks, Paul noticed his enemy walking to the men's room. He said, "The coast is clear, my dears. I must away to the Bryson while I have a chance."

As he got up from the booth, Gregorio asked, "Should you be driving home in your condition?"

"Touching of you to ask, but this is my neighborhood bar. The walk here is my daily exercise. Lovely to meet you two," he said to Moira and Bernie. "And I'm sure I'll be seeing you other gentlemen soon." He blew a kiss to us as he made his way to the door.

Once Paul left, I told Winston I was sorry for having disparaged his punk name, and he responded, "No need to apologize. I know very well that I am a little absurd." After a lull in the conversation, we decided to leave the bar. Moira offered to drive Bernie home, and I took Gregorio's keys.

On the way to the truck, we saw a pile of discarded toilets in front of an apartment building being renovated. We walked a little farther, then I turned around and said, "Hey, hold on. I think I can use those toilets for something."

Gregorio moaned, "You want to load them into my truck?"

"Don't worry, I only want a few, and if they're too shitty, we won't bother."

Winston, Gregorio, and I each carried a toilet, and I ran back and took a fourth one. Weighed down with all that porcelain, the truck lumbered along the streets leading to the Hollywood Freeway, past the neighborhood where I would be living in a few months. I drove slowly, stayed in the right lane, and let cars honk at us. After about fifty minutes, we reached Cal Arts, where I unloaded the toilets into my studio. Winston led Gregorio, who was about to pass out, to his studio to sleep.

∞

From the time I first moved to California, I promised myself that I'd never see my mother during Christmastime. The cold weather combined with compulsory good cheer made me even more depressed than I'd normally be when visiting the Midwestern wasteland where I grew up. My experience of living in Los Angeles was so radically different from what I left behind that I was amazed I didn't need a passport when I landed at the airport. Not just the climate, but the whole social environment came as a shock. California was the place where people had the freedom to reinvent themselves. My hometown was where I would have ended up living if I hadn't had the motivation and ingenuity to escape. During my childhood, factory workers without college degrees could make reasonably comfortable livings and raise families. By the time I was an adolescent, the economy had begun to fail these people. Some of their children found ways to invent new lives for themselves during the first flush of punk rock in America. That was twenty years before, and other possibilities had failed to materialize in the interim. Any young person who didn't leave my hometown to attend university got stuck in a region where the real estate remained dirt cheap because no one wanted to move there.

My mother hadn't ever lived more than ten miles away from where she was born. Her world had never been very big, but after my father's death, it contracted even more. I would try to explain how I survived and what I studied, but these were things so far beyond her understanding that she passed over what I said in silence. Conversation became impossible. At one point, when I was complaining about my finances, she told me, "You can always move back home if you need to."

"Los Angeles is where I belong," I said as calmly as I could. "My time there isn't some kind of vacation. If all goes well, I'll be there for the rest of my life." She gave me a puzzled look, as though I had said something in a foreign language. A couple of days later, I flew back home.

∞

I had heard that there was a sex club near Moira's apartment, but I didn't find out exactly where until the second time I stayed at her place. I decided to visit it on New Year's Eve. I paid for a membership and checked my clothes, then entered the dark, disorienting environment. The acrid smell, a combination of disinfectant, poppers, and excrement, assaulted me. As my eyes got used to the darkness, I could make out naked male figures. Some of them had erections. One was passed out in a sling while a line of guys took turns fucking him. I noticed a number of men at the margins of the space masturbating. They might have been rubbing their penises in solitude for hours. Whatever drug they were doing isolated them from their fellow sex club patrons. I found the sight very disturbing. After a couple of circuits around the place, I put my clothes on and left. I thought I saw Bernie out of the corner of my eye, arriving as I was leaving. Now I had a notion of where the sex life he never talked about was played out.

I realized that it wasn't only sex that I craved, but intimacy. On a whim, I decided to call my friend Daniel, whom I'd fisted years before. He picked up the phone and I wished him a happy New Year. I should have known better than to call him on a holiday. There was so much noise in the background that he could barely hear me. I tried to have a conversation with him, but he told me that his boyfriend was listening and another time would be better. I gave him Moira's number and said I'd be there for the rest of the week. I knew he'd never call me back.

SEVENTEEN

When the library reopened on the first day of spring semester, I wrote to Temo wishing him a happy New Year. I had little hope that he'd respond. I concluded that he was a lost soul struggling to understand something, and he drew a bunch people into his personal drama. He couldn't help himself.

A day later, I got the following response to my email: "Sorry if I hurt you and Moira. I'm confused. I married my friend Julieta. She knows everything about me and loves me anyway. I fucked up my life. Forgive me. Maybe I'll see you again one day. Thinking of you, Temo."

∞

My main challenge for the next couple of months was figuring out what to do with the toilets that I had brought into my studio, after scrubbing them so they weren't a biohazard. From Moira I heard that Lenin had written about toilets, and I was intrigued. I tried to find the reference in various bibliographies and the

Reader's Guide to Periodical Literature without any luck, because no one had thought to cross reference the first leader of the USSR with plumbing. I asked Winston, but he was no help. James Benning, whom I knew from the Film Today class, suggested I try an internet search engine, something I had never used before. On a computer in the library, I found AltaVista, typed "Lenin" and "toilet" into the window, and clicked "search." I came up with nothing, then I started using other search terms: urinal, bathroom, lavatory. The results for the last one included a link to the Marxist Internet Archive. Its website collected translations of texts by Marx and Engels and other communists, including an essay called "The Importance of Gold Now and After the Complete Victory of Socialism," written by V. I. Lenin on November 5, 1921, and published the next day in *Pravda*. It included the following sentence: "When we are victorious on a world scale I think we shall use gold for the purpose of building public lavatories in the streets of some of the largest cities of the world." I couldn't have been happier with my discovery.

Transforming discarded toilets into the golden fixtures of Lenin's dream was more difficult than I anticipated. I received a grant from the Art School to buy gold leaf, but applying it to slippery white porcelain proved to be impossible. One instructor suggested I paint the toilets a matte red, the traditional base for making gold appear brighter and warmer. I would have to do tests to see which type of paint would work best, but in principle, my problem was solved.

I called Frances, and she laughed when I told her about my experiments. She said, "You're becoming a painter. I knew it would happen eventually."

"Red toilets in the service of the glorious communist revolution." I asked her, "How do you like New York?"

"I'm happy I moved here. For one thing, there are more women to sleep with. I like Brooklyn, too. Williamsburg is a dump, but it's convenient, and I have a big place."

"Are you working?"

"I'm cooking for a living right now, but I want to find adjunct teaching work. One day, I'll get a studio. Painting at home is impossible, at least the way I do it."

"Well, we miss you here. The first year MFA students are really awful, just like the Pack on *Buffy, the Vampire Slayer*."

"Ah, *Buffy*. Well, don't sit around and complain. Make your own fun."

"That's good advice. I'll be sure to tell Winston and Gregorio."

"How are you boys doing?"

"Oh, fine. Winston missed registration. We were afraid he might not show up at all. He and Gregorio are a serious couple now. They live together in Saugus."

"Is Winston making work?"

"He's taking a cue from you and working on a large painting."

"I want to see your thesis shows. What week are you installing?"

"The week before spring break, same as you did."

"It's a bitch, but once it's over, you'll be so relieved."

∞

Winston finally showed me his work in progress. It reinterpreted Lawrence Alma-Tadema's Victorian-era painting, *The Roses of Heliogabalus*, which depicts the smothering of dinner guests in a huge pile of rose petals by the capricious and sadistic Roman emperor Elagabalus. In the original, the falling petals, which take up most of the painting's surface, are rendered as painstakingly as possible, while in Winston's version, the field of pink and red looked more like a membrane of human flesh with livid, bloody chunks protruding. The androgynous and decadent Romans in the original were replaced by Albanian men in sober, ill-fitting bureaucratic suits. The sumptuous villa of patterned marble and polished wood became a modern boardroom in the socialist style; and the artworks in the background were transformed from classical statuary into socialist realist paintings of Enver Hoxha. His successor, Ramiz Alia, whom I recognized from the news stories I had read over the summer, sat unscathed at a table above the fray, with an ecstatic look on his face.

I looked closely at the painting and asked, "Is it done?"

"Almost. I think it is too sweet. I want my paintings to look like acts of violence, not nice figurative art. I was taught socialist realism when I was a child, and I know how to paint that way. When I first saw abstract art, it was a shock. I knew it existed, but to see an abstract painting up close in a museum—for me it was like being torn apart from the inside. In every painting I want to reproduce that feeling of being torn apart."

"Damn, you're writing your artist's statement. You'll be a good interview subject." Winston looked perplexed, and I said, "I should be taking notes." I scanned his studio and noticed many paintings stashed away. "Will anyone see these?"

"I don't know. I think no one cares about such things anymore."

"Your paintings have to make them care."

"Good point," he said, as he got back to work.

∞

Winston and I installed our shows in two adjacent galleries, the Lime and the Mint, named for the colors of their front doors. They had been built on the mezzanine over the Main Gallery after the Northridge earthquake. They were small, but they had good lighting and new, relatively unblemished walls that didn't reach all the way up to the ceiling. Winston's big painting barely fit the space. He also hung two of his portraits, Mao and Stalin. It wasn't possible to step back a long way from the work, and the effect was overpowering. The year before, Frances had done large-scale paintings, but as far as I knew, no one had done a thesis exhibition of such ambition since then. My own show looked a bit anemic by comparison. At least there was adequate space for the gold toilets, all four of them, in a line along the back wall. I wanted to include the Lenin essay that inspired the pieces, so I had the text typeset and printed. I found a pedestal and placed a pile of copies on it by the door; spectators could take one as they left.

The next day, as I unlocked the gallery, I noticed a stench. I found a small turd in one of the toilets. "What the fuck?!" I yelled. I immediately went to the Art School office and announced to anyone who'd listen that my thesis show had been defaced before it had even opened. The administrative assistant made a call, and we went to the gallery. One security guard came to take Polaroid pictures and get a statement from me. Another wore long rubber gloves and removed the offending object from the toilet. I grabbed cleaning supplies and more gold leaf from my studio. I spent the rest of the morning repairing the damage, and I did a pretty good job of it, though a smell lingered. Winston came by later to open his gallery, and I told him what had happened. He laughed then apologized for laughing. He checked his paintings, and was relieved to see that the vandal had done nothing to them. The odor was masked by the smell of drying oil paint. I went back to the Art School office to let people know that I did my best to repair the damage and that Winston's work was unharmed. I was ushered into a meeting with the dean, who assured me that the Art School would do whatever it could to catch the culprit.

A while later, I was called into another meeting, since without much effort, security had discovered who had shit on my work. It was one of the Pack, not Brad the leader—though I imagined the prank had been his idea—but Jerry, whose drunken advances I had spurned. It was a bad week for him. The costs of a recent drunk driving conviction were starting to dawn on him. He hadn't made any art that semester, and this was reflected in his grades, as well as the scholarship he was given by the Art School. I figured the guy had enough problems, and I didn't wish to add to them. An apology was enough for me.

∞

I heard that Jerry wasn't the only member of the Pack to receive a paltry scholarship. His friends loudly complained that the school had failed to recognize their talent, while refusing to admit that the evidence of it was minimal. Brad, who never took the activities of the clique very seriously despite being at the center of them, had played the game well enough that he got a reasonable financial aid package, but he let his followers get screwed. As he saw it, they had only themselves to blame for not having done any work and spending all their money on drugs. The Pack threatened to drop out of school en masse, but none of them did, because they knew that Cal Arts was one of the few places in the world where anyone would give such lazy and self-involved artists so much as the time of day.

Gregorio, who was a semester behind Winston and me and would not graduate until December, indirectly benefited from the misfortunes of the Pack. He received a full scholarship for his last semester, partly because the faculty came to understand his strengths as an artist, and partly because there was extra money freed up by the debacle of the first year MFA students. Others who had not been members of the clique also benefited, and students insulted by these would-be art stars felt a sense of vindication.

∞

The visiting artist coordinator had heard that François Werner, the director of a Swiss *kunsthalle* and widely regarded as a force in the art world, would be in Los Angeles for a job interview. After protracted negotiations, Werner committed to coming to campus for a lecture and studio visits. His visit coincided with the week of my thesis show and Winston's. I signed up for a meeting with him and convinced Winston to do the same.

Werner comported himself professionally when visiting studios, though he didn't seem thrilled to be doing so. The last two meetings were with Winston and me. I went first. He noticed a lingering smell in the gallery, and I explained what had happened. I handed him a copy of the Lenin essay, and he gave the text no more than a cursory glance, then took a look at the gold toilets. His attention wandered almost immediately. He said, "The odor is the best part of the exhibition. This reminds me of John Miller's work. Have you seen it?"

"Only in reproduction."

"I believe he did a lot of gold leafed excrement. You should look it up." He handed back the Lenin text and said, "His writing about art is also very good."

"Thanks for the reference."

"Of course, there is a psychoanalytic, as opposed to a Marxist, reading for this work. I'm sure you're aware of that, but I think John has gone farther along these lines than you have." He peered at me and said, "You're an American. Why do you care about Lenin?"

No one had ever asked me that question, and I struggled to find an answer. "I think the society where gold is so worthless that it's used to manufacture toilets must be a kind of utopia. Obviously, this utopia never came into existence, but that doesn't mean we should stop hoping for it."

"Hope?" His interest was piqued. "Isn't that a bit naïve?"

"Is it? If you forget about utopia, you may as well go into another business. Why make art at all?"

He responded, "There are plenty of other reasons to make art. Only today, I heard quite a few of them."

"I realize my concerns are unfashionable…"

"To say the least. It's as if 1989 never happened. But that's the project's most charming aspect." He gestured toward the pile of papers. "You don't need the historical apparatus. The work is better without you pointing at things."

"I see. Well, I'm at school, and texts seem necessary."

"Unfortunately." He looked around, at a loss to say more. "Are you sure you're an artist?"

I was taken aback. "No, not entirely. I started out as a writer."

"That explains the text, then."

"Yes." I thought for a moment. "I'm not very comfortable with the physical labor that painters seem to enjoy. I came to Cal Arts because of its reputation as a place to do conceptual art. I'm not sure that's the case anymore."

"Well, your thoughts on these questions are more advanced than your fellow students, I can say that. Good luck." He turned to go.

I called after him, "Thank you."

I noticed that Winston had been standing outside the gallery waiting. He led Werner to his show, and the two of them started to speak in German. I went back to my studio to give them some privacy and to think about what had been said to me.

When Winston returned, I asked him how the meeting with Werner had gone, and he said, "Very well. He wants to give me an exhibition."

"That's great," I said. "Congratulations. What did he say about the paintings?"

"A lot. He suggested that I use my real name for art after I graduate. Being Albanian is something I should be proud of, and Europeans will be curious about someone from the Balkans."

I asked, "What's your full name, by the way?"

"Andë Alia."

"Are you related to the man in your painting, Ramiz Alia?"

"Not closely, but yes."

"That's why it was safe for you to be a punk in East Berlin." I asked, "Was the story of your forced expatriation made up?"

"Not exactly. Yes, I was punk trash dumped in West Berlin by drunken policemen. I did receive 'welcome money' and help from a social worker. No one knew how to deal with this odd person who resembled a guest worker from Turkey or Greece, but spoke perfect German. All citizens of the East automatically received citizenship in the West, but this rule only applied to refugees who were German 'by blood'—a distinction made in the official documents of the Federal Republic even today. Thanks to this rule instituted by the Nazis, my immigration status was ambiguous. I had no proof that I was a citizen of the German Democratic Republic, but they had no proof that I was not. If I had claimed the status of defector, I would have been treated better, but there would also have been an obligation to debrief me, as you say in English. The intelligence services would have put me under close surveillance. I said nothing and hoped. I did not make use of my diplomatic status. I assume the Stasi knew where I was. My family did not. I thought it was too dangerous to call them or even to write a post card." Winston was fighting off tears. "When the political situation seemed safe, I made inquiries, and learned that my father had died, and my mother and sister had returned home. I talked to them on the phone, but I never visited them. When officials of socialist Albania, including members of my family, were put on trial by the new government, I thought it best to stay away indefinitely. Anyone with the name Alia was automatically under suspicion."

I asked, "How did you manage to solve your money problems over the summer?"

"This is the dishonorable part of my story. You see, I missed the deadlines to apply for a proper scholarship from Germany. I called Uncle Ramiz and begged for his help. I had no other choice. I was lucky, he was able to do something. Soon after, I was informed of a bank account set up in my name with a substantial balance.

No one would object if I withdrew tuition money. I still have access to this account, and I notice that funds go in and come out on a constant basis."

"Money laundering," I said tentatively.

"You are correct. This is currently the main economic activity of capitalist Albania. Perhaps it was the main economic activity of socialist Albania, too."

I said, "So the privileged elite of the old regime has become the privileged elite of the new one."

He shrugged. "I have not seen this with my own eyes, but yes, that would be a reasonable assumption. Uncle Ramiz went to prison for misappropriating state funds, and after two years was released. Then there was another trial, for crimes against humanity, and he was sentenced again. He went to prison, but escaped when the prison guards deserted in the chaos of the civil war. He is now arranging permanent residency in Dubai."

I was astonished by all the new information about my friend. I could only think to ask, "Would the name Alia mean anything to people in the art world?"

He said, "I doubt it. Only to Albanians, and to you. But as far as I can determine, no one can denounce Ramiz Alia's supposed crimes without appearing hypocritical. I understand that money laundering is the main animating force not only of my native country, but of the art market in the West. Perhaps I will feel perfectly at home in this new realm of capitalist manipulation."

I laughed. "Well, at least you've solved the Dead Kennedys problem. Winston Smith is dead. Long live Andë Alia. It has a nice ring to it."

After this rather involved speech, which he had probably prepared, he said, "I forgot to ask about your meeting."

"It was only so-so. Werner can be quite critical. I think my obsessions are uncharacteristic of an American, and since they don't fit a curator's preconceived ideas, they're unwelcome."

Winston frowned. "Europeans want every American artist to be Iggy Pop."

"I guess that's one explanation for the prodigious success of Mike Kelley."

Winston asked me not to tell anyone about his meeting with Werner. This seemed wise. The "good old days" of art world luminaries paying attention to Cal Arts thesis exhibitions were long gone, and if anyone found out that a curator offered Winston a show at a prestigious European venue, there would have been something like a panic in the Art School. I pictured the Pack becoming enraged at the idea of Winston rather than them receiving this kind of validation. My fellow students were as careerist as they had ever been, but they lacked the practical skills to pull off a brilliant gambit just out of school. For most of us, it would be a groping and haphazard path toward a life as an artist. Winston was being given a rare opportunity, and he wanted to take full advantage of it, unmolested by the envy of his fellow students, many of whom were consumed by petty, soulless ambition.

EIGHTEEN

Winston shut himself up in his studio during the period when most students were relaxing and getting sentimental about graduating. He also changed his appearance. His wardrobe became more conventional and subdued, and his hair color returned to dark brown. He seemed to paint non-stop, with breaks only to sleep with Gregorio and have occasional late night conversations with me.

He showed me a new painting. Rather than a portrait of a dictator beset by pox, it was an image of an architectural wreck in the approximate shape of a pyramid. It looked like the cover illustration of a pulp science fiction novel from the 1960s—the past's prediction of a future that never arrived. I asked, "Does this actually exist?"

He said, "You have never seen the Pyramid of Tirana."

"No, when was it built?"

"After Enver Hoxha's death in 1985, as a monument to him. It is now a ruin, thirteen years later." He gestured toward the painting. "A pyramid is the perfect symbol for a dictatorship. The leader occupies one point at the top and stands on the base of the masses.

It is appropriate that the Egyptians with their god kings invented the structure."

"It describes a confidence game, too." I asked, "Didn't Albania fall victim to pyramid schemes?"

Winston chuckled. "A wonderful coincidence." He paused. "Not so wonderful for those who invested. But yes, the pyramid symbolizes many of Albania's problems, and it is extraordinarily ugly. Hideous is the word, I think."

"Hideous does it justice," I said as I gazed at the painting again.

He said, "You know, Americans have their pyramid schemes, too. Art school, for example." I turned and saw a smile on his face.

"Explain what you mean."

"You were surprised by François Werner's critical remarks because you rarely hear such things. The dominant mode of discourse in this school is affirmative. As long as instructors are supportive, the students do not drop out. They feel encouraged, and they continue to pay their tuition; thus the institution can continue to exist. But why does it exist? Many thousands of art students graduate every year. There is no place for them in society. They have been sold a fictional future, based on what Americans call wishful thinking. This is rather immoral, yet as long as money flows through the system, the pyramid remains standing. Am I not right?"

I was stunned. I hadn't ever thought of art education as an outright scam. I asked, "Has your experience here been worthless?"

"On the contrary, but my best experiences have nothing to do with school per se. Must we pay a lot of money to meet friends and lovers, curators and critics? It is very corrupt, I think."

∞

Winston's criticisms were never far from my thoughts in those days. During his brief time at art school, he had figured out the whole system, and I was curious to see how he would apply his analytical skills to a wider world. One day, I asked him about the art market. In response, he laid out his strategy: "After a brief flirtation with 'political art' during the slump of the early 1990s, the market has rebounded and is now dominated by nostalgia; therefore, I must insert myself into the canon of Western art. I will emphasize my virtuosity, because bourgeois collectors only admire art that they are incapable of making themselves."

I scoffed, "You sound like you want to bring back French academic painting."

"No, I will do the only kind of painting I can do, in my own style, and draw inspiration from my life. Not the East Berlin punk, but the son of an Albanian diplomat. I will paint the drama of totalitarianism in the twentieth century."

"Isn't Albania difficult to sell to people who can't even find it on the map?"

"I will sell myself as a creature from the exotic East, which is poor, troubled, bloody, undemocratic. The Western bourgeois is undemocratic, too, but he forgets about this when confronted with his opposite, a man of the Balkans. I will offer collectors images that confirm their sense of superiority."

I asked, "Do you have the stomach for that?"

"I was not born with the choices that Americans have. I learned to make the best of a situation that cannot be changed. If I am destined to be colonized, I will colonize myself."

"But you rebelled once, when you became a punk."

"That was a childish pose, and does not fit the correct *biografi*, so I will revise." He used the word for the family history by which everyone in socialist Albania used to be judged: proletarians were privileged, while people from bourgeois families lived with a stigma they couldn't escape. Outside his native country, he could invent a new *biografi*, something that Albanians under Enver Hoxha were unable to do.

I paused to reflect on what Winston was saying. It made sense, but it struck me as cynical. Instead of challenging him on matters of principle, I asked, "Do you think your strategy will work?"

"It is already working. I have exhibitions scheduled for the fall and winter. There is what you call a buzz. I must not disappoint."

I nodded and said, "This is your chance."

"It is good that you understand."

"Where will you live?"

"Certainly not Los Angeles. It is too far from Europe and not miserable enough."

"Tirana?" I asked.

"Too miserable. I would risk being beaten to death as a homosexual, and anyway, one cannot even buy decent art supplies there. East Berlin, I think. When I visited, it was like home, certainly more so than this desert. International architects are now transforming Potsdamer Platz into the ugliest place on earth, but farther from the center there are still cheap places where artists can work."

"Will you take Gregorio along with you?"

"Of course, if he wants. I love him. He is a good person."

"I hope you'll be happy."

Winston laughed. "Happiness? This is an illusion. But I will make great paintings." At that moment, I saw a strange expression come across Winston's face. It was as though he had become an old man before my eyes. He said, "I must return to work. There is so much to do."

I said, "Before I go, I have to tell you, I've been thinking about your idea of art school as pyramid scheme. It's true that our judgments about art are often wrong, and students and faculty pay attention to words more than pictures. Good talkers do well here, and I suppose I'm an example of that. There's also an atmosphere that encourages a kind of popularity contest; appearances are everything. But I'm convinced that ultimately, hard work will be rewarded. I see it happening for you. That's the opposite of corruption."

Winston rubbed his chin and nodded. "A typically American response, worthy of Henry Ford or Thomas Edison—the capitalist gangsters who espoused the virtue of hard work. Perhaps you are right. You should come to Berlin. You can correct my errors in logic. I will miss you most of all."

Soon after our talk, I began to see people visiting Winston at odd hours. They arrived in expensive cars that idled outside the studios while the meetings took place. Sometimes they talked in English, sometimes in German. Since I was in the adjoining studio, I heard bits and pieces of the conversations. I peeked in and saw Winston showing works that no one on campus had seen. Sometimes the visitors would leave with a painting, carrying it gingerly, as it would still be wet.

∞

The last weeks of the semester, which should have been joyous for us, became fraught with doubts and anxieties. One day I saw Gregorio sobbing in his studio. I asked him what was wrong, and he answered, "Winston is definitely moving to Berlin. He asked me to join him when I graduate."

"That sounds great. Why not?"

He frowned. "Well, I don't speak German, for one thing. And the time I've spent in Europe hasn't been that great."

"Living in a place isn't the same as being a tourist."

He nodded, then asked, "Did I tell you I went to Russia on a school trip?"

"Never."

"Parts of it were fun, but it was scary, too. Near the end of our stay, we were at a café in Moscow, and I saw an older guy staring at me. He was pretty sexy. I was still a teenager, and I felt really uncomfortable, but excited, too. He took my teacher aside and asked her, 'Is he Indian?' because lot of people from India visited Russia in Soviet times. She said, 'No, he's Mexican,' and the man got much more interested. She told me later that he wanted to 'buy' me from her for a night, or maybe to take me as his kept boy. He was a gangster, and he assumed any teacher could be convinced to pimp out her students if the price was right."

I could hardly believe what I was hearing. "What happened?"

"When he found out we were all American citizens, he backed down. Too much trouble. Maybe he thought the price would be too high. I don't know. Anyway, I still think about that guy. I was sitting close enough to him to know that he never used deodorant. He was sort of horrible, but I sometimes wonder what my life would have been like if I became the plaything of an Eastern European thug."

I broke the mood by laughing loudly. "I guess you've found your lover from the East after all."

Gregorio rolled his eyes. "I don't think about Winston that way. Next thing, you'll be saying I want to fuck my father."

"Don't you?"

"You're the worst. But at least you cheered me up a little."

I said, "I'll be sad to see you leave. My hopes for another three-way with you two have definitely gone out the window."

"You never quit, do you? Winston was all for it, but I was the one who said no."

"I figured that was the case."

"It's bad enough that Winston talks about you constantly. He really respects you. I wouldn't want to compete with you in bed, too. Your personality is too domineering. If you controlled the situation, I know you'd try to take Winston away from me."

I protested, "I don't think so."

"You like him better than me. I understand. I like him better than me, too."

"I like you both. I backed off because I didn't want to lose you as friends."

Gregorio looked as if he would cry at any moment. "You don't know how hard it is. I don't fit into the gay world. I'm short and brown, and white guys don't pay any attention to me. My trips to gay bars have been disasters."

"That's common enough. Most bars are awful."

He said, "I've lost so many times in my life. I want to win just this once."

With a tone of bitterness I couldn't conceal, I said, "Hey, if you think this is a contest, I was the loser from the start." I looked up and noticed the time. "I have an appointment. See you later."

I went from one tense discussion to another: my exit interview with the financial aid office, where I discovered the consequences of the loans to which I had blithely agreed at the beginning of each academic year. My total indebtedness was around $20,000, not bad for a student of my generation at a private art school, but more than I envisioned being able to repay. I taped the paper explaining my new financial obligations to the wall of my studio, as a reminder of the cost of a two year vacation from adulthood.

∞

Cal Arts prided itself on its unconventional and informal graduation ceremonies, which were immensely long and drawn out, because every graduating student was allowed to make a speech or stage some kind of performance when receiving a diploma. By mid-May, it was already very hot in Santa Clarita. The combination of brutal sunshine, boring speeches, and grossly excessive alcohol consumption had a ghastly effect on the Class of 1998. I was surprised that there wasn't more vomit, but I supposed people kept themselves from falling apart while their parents were around and didn't get truly messy until late at night. The spectacle was enough to make me swear off alcohol for the whole day, if not for the rest of my life.

The day after graduation, a truck from an art handling company showed up at Winston's studio. Movers crated his paintings and placed them carefully inside compartments specially designed for transporting works of art. I asked Winston where his paintings were going, and he said they would be in an exhibition at a New York gallery. Once he arrived in Berlin, he would find a studio and make a whole new body of work for his European exhibition. I hugged and congratulated him.

"I have something to show you," he said as the hug came to an end. We stood in front of the first painting he completed at school, the portrait of Enver Hoxha, hanging alone on the wall next to the door. He said, "It is yours if you want it."

"Of course I do, but isn't this supposed to go to a gallery?" I asked.

"You should own it. You had faith in my painting when no one else would talk to me. You insisted I meet with Werner. And you fucked me in the ass when I needed it." We both smiled. I took the painting down and placed it in my studio. Winston followed me with a cardboard box. It contained items he couldn't take to Berlin: old books and a few souvenirs. I asked him if he'd need any of these things, and he responded, "I can buy everything again. Berlin has a giant flea market, selling the refuse of the socialist East. You must come visit. You will love it."

Winston looked around my nearly empty studio and noticed the loan form on the wall. I said, "That's my introduction to debt peonage, courtesy of the American educational system."

He said, "A fucking scandal. If Gregorio moves to Berlin, he can stop paying. But then he cannot return to the United States." He took a small bottle of *raki* from the box. "I was saving this for a special occasion. Now we have no more occasions. We finish the bottle." As though materialized by a wish, Gregorio appeared to join us. Winston poured three glasses of *raki*, then added a bit of water, which turned the liquid cloudy. He said, "This is tiger's milk."

I made a toast: "To the future." We clinked our glasses and drank the tiger's milk in one gulp. I tried not to embarrass myself by choking on what tasted to me like anise-flavored lighter fluid.

∞

The next day, Winston was gone. Gregorio and I made the best of things in his absence. I told him, "Anyone can leave us at any time. We should appreciate what we have."

"I agree," he said. With a tactlessness I hoped was endearing, I asked Gregorio if he could help me move. "If I didn't love you so much I'd tell you to fuck off." I smiled because he had never told me he loved me before.

We loaded most of the contents of my studio into his truck. After salvaging what I could of the gold leaf, which, contrary to Lenin's prediction, still had value, I threw the toilets I used for my thesis exhibition into a dumpster. I figured that since the show had been documented, I didn't really need the actual objects anymore. We drove to Moira's, and she gave me a copy of her key. Once I had carried my boxes into the apartment, she proposed that we have dinner at Don Felix, and we happily agreed. As we waited for a table, she asked, "Where's Winston?" I explained his departure and mentioned that although we still called him by that name, henceforth, he would be known to the rest of the world as Andë Alia.

Moira asked, "Any relation to Ramiz Alia?"

"Winston's great uncle," I said, thinking that we were possibly the only two people in the United States at that moment talking about Enver Hoxha's successor. "He has a financial lifeline there, but as far as I can tell, our friend's hands are clean."

"Albania is a horrible mess these days," Moira said with a shudder. "No more war zones for me."

"Where are you going?" we asked her, almost in unison.

"Well, first to my parents' house, then to Mexico. I won't get a PhD yet. I have a job teaching Spanish in Chiapas."

"Isn't that a war zone?" I asked.

"You really should read the news," she said. "An armistice was signed last year."

Gregorio asked, "Isn't Spanish your second language?"

She replied, "It's the students' second language, too. I'll be at a school for indigenous people. They're the majority of the population in that part of Mexico. A referendum on indigenous rights is scheduled for next year."

"The radical will never die." I said, "I'm happy for you. I hope it works out."

"Since I'm leaving, I can put in a good word for you at Libros Revolución. You already know the stock, and it wouldn't hurt you to improve your Spanish. Bernie is still working there, so it might be nice."

"Nicer than Videoactive, I'm sure. I'll make a better employee than dear old Temo, anyway." Moira looked a bit wounded at the mention of his name, and I immediately said, "I'm sorry."

"Oh, I'm just being a fool." There was a pause. "Have you heard from him?"

I said, "No, but he has my number now, since I'll be taking over your line. It wouldn't surprise me one bit if he found marital bliss less than satisfactory and started calling." Gregorio looked curious, but I didn't feel like explaining things. My affair with Temo was firmly in the past as far as I knew. I asked Gregorio, "Will you be spending the summer here or in New Mexico?"

He said, "Here. I want to work in my studio. Winston gave me lots of art supplies before he left. I'm going to try painting in oils, like my friends do."

"And what about Berlin?"

"I don't know yet. I sometimes think he'll drop me as soon as he gets famous."

"I doubt it. He really loves you." Gregorio nodded at this, and a tear formed in his eye.

∞

After Moira left the apartment for good and Gregorio retreated to his studio to paint, I was alone in my new home. I sent out change of address forms and called a few people to inform them of my phone number. Within days I got my first piece of mail: a notice concerning my student loans.

I had only a diploma, which I received in the mail after graduation, a couple of videos, and slides of my gold toilets to show for my time in art school. I felt like the characters on *The Simpsons*, who in every episode would go on crazy adventures, then twenty-two minutes later, would end up exactly as they were at the beginning. "Well, almost," I said to myself. I thought about what had changed in me, and I instinctively reached for a pad and pen. With no assignment, no deadlines, and no idea of where it would lead, I started to write. As the sun set, I looked at my work and saw that I had several pages of text. I said to myself, "I should turn on a light." And once I did, I continued writing.

NINETEEN

I started working at Libros Revolución, which was a half hour walk from my new apartment. As Moira predicted, my Spanish got better on the job. I was also able to read during the many quiet hours I spent at the counter. The manager disapproved of my taste in fiction, but I didn't give him any trouble, so he had no real reason to complain. He enlisted me to clear out the back room after he discovered the can of Crisco that Temo had used for fisting sessions; his groan of disgust indicated that he had some idea as to why it was there. I didn't mind the grunt work, because it gave me an opportunity to learn about Temo's secret life. As instructed, I disposed of all the unnecessary items, but a few books and posters found their way into my apartment.

While we were working together one day, Bernie announced, "I'm planning to leave town soon." This surprised me, because I expected him to stay forever. I had come to understand Los Angeles as a whirlpool, drawing people in and subjecting them to forces that would eventually suck them down the drain. When a new arrival reached a certain point, moving away became impossible.

"Are you going to take your collections with you?" I asked, remembering how many boxes I'd seen in his apartment.

"Only a few things. The rest will go into storage." Trying to make the best of a bad situation, he said, "A hot, dry environment preserved the Gnostic gospels for over a thousand years. Maybe my books will be safer here."

"And you'll have a reason to return."

He asked me to meet him at his apartment later in the week, and, knowing this was out of character, he explained, "I want to show you some things."

∞

I took the bus and arrived at Bernie's shortly after eleven a. m., before the worst heat of the day. We were enjoying "June gloom," a period of cloudy skies in the morning followed by bright sunshine in the afternoon. Because of the temporary respite it provided from punishing temperatures, those overcast June days were my favorite time of year. Tourists expecting sunny California were disappointed by the phenomenon, and that made me like it even more.

Bernie's apartment seemed nearly as crowded as the last time I had been there, but he had imposed an order on the boxes, which were arranged in neat rows. There was enough room for me to walk comfortably to the back wall, where he had hung a group of photographs. I wondered if anyone had seen the inside of Bernie's apartment since my visit early in our friendship. Perhaps innumerable tricks had traipsed in and out of the Art Deco building on Ambrose Avenue to serve Bernie's sexual needs. Somehow I doubted it.

He announced, "This is part of the Brian Weil study collection, the prints I set aside while I worked for him." I gravitated to the first photograph in the line, which depicted a naked man in a sinuous pose seen from the side against a very dark background. One foot stepped in front of the other, and the shoulders were slightly hunched. The model's head was bent down and covered by a black ski mask, the outlines of which could only be seen in contrast to a white square (possibly a window) in the background. It was impossible to tell if the eyes behind the mask were open or closed. If they were open, they looked directly at the enormous erect penis held in the model's right hand.

I asked, "Do you know who this is?"

"It's Brian's naked body, but it's not his penis. I'm fairly certain the dildo he used for this photo was the one I found while cleaning his darkroom long after the fact. Years in a damp basement and exposure to various kinds of photo chemistry and who knows what else had taken its toll. It did *not* enter my study collection."

"Is it a self-portrait?"

Bernie was quick to respond, "Absolutely not. In his classes, Brian had an ongoing diatribe against anything of the sort. It basically wasn't allowed. Students at ICP would invariably present work with narratives like, 'Each year I take a nude self-portrait.' That brought up torrents of insults from him."

I smiled. I was happy that Bernie saw fit to show me what were possibly the most valuable items in his collection, or at least the most secret. The photographs had a dated feel—a lamentable attention to fashion had crept into my recent art school graduate's outlook—and even though Brian had been dead for only a couple of years, it seemed to me that he already belonged to a distant past. Instead of bringing this up, I asked about the visual texture of the work. The prints were contrasty and lacked detail, which I assumed aided the fakery necessary to make them.

Bernie explained, "Brian had worked out a way of rephotographing conventional black and white negatives and super-eight film footage. His 'a-ha!' moment was seeing a picture of David Berkowitz after he had been caught and was being kept under wraps. On its front page, the *Post* ran an indistinct image shot through a small grimy window with the headline 'Son of Sam Sleeps!' I often thought that should be researched—if it really happened or not. It's a good story." He took a break and sipped a glass of weak lemonade that I suspected was spiked with vodka.

I reflected on what was missing, what Bernie saw in the work that I didn't. I came to the conclusion that there was no possibility of objectivity in the matter. An aura surrounded Brian, and anyone who didn't have direct personal experience of his charisma would lack a crucial part of the picture. There was an unbridgeable gap of emotion. At that moment, I realized that Brian was the love of Bernie's life. How Brian responded to this love I would never know. The thought that this great passion could have been unrequited brought tears to my eyes.

I fumbled in my bag and brought out the *Helter Skelter* catalogue, lent to me on that very spot over two years before. I said, "I need to return this." Bernie, unaccustomed to showing his feelings around others, was relieved by the change of subject. He offered to drive me home, and on the way, we spontaneously decided to stop at a Thai restaurant neither of us had tried. Over lunch, the morning's discussion didn't come up. We had a relaxed and pleasant meal.

∞

One evening, I came home and sensed a presence in my apartment. With my hand on the doorknob, ready to escape, I shouted, "Hello?" Out of the shadows stepped Temo. He had just taken a shower and was dripping wet, wrapped in a towel. I couldn't believe what I was seeing and approached to touch him and confirm that he wasn't a hallucination. He dropped the towel and began to kiss me. I took off my clothes as quickly as I could, and we went into the bedroom, where I fucked him. I was so excited that I didn't last very long and quickly came in his ass with a violent spurt. He rolled onto his back and jerked off until he came soon afterward. We collapsed on the bed and fell asleep in each other's arms.

I woke up first and gathered my clothes from the living room. I heard Temo stirring and went back to bed. He turned over and said, "You snore."

"You didn't know that because we didn't sleep together."

"I never slept with anyone." I wanted to ask him a hundred questions, but I decided to wait for him to do the talking. He rubbed his eyes and said, "My hole is tight again. No fists."

"Is that why I came so quickly?"

"Because you needed sex. Me too."

I couldn't resist asking, "Where have you been?"

"I need coffee." He walked into the kitchen naked, and after some rummaging around in the cabinets, he found a coffee pot. A while later, he came back with a cup.

"You've made yourself at home. How did you get in?"

"Somebody forgot to change the locks. Remember, I had a copy of Moira's key."

I scratched my head and said, "Oh, that's right. I hope you didn't share it with any of your tricks."

He gave me a contemptuous glance. "Why do you have to say such a thing?"

I asked, "What happened in Mexico?"

He took a long time to formulate an answer as he sipped his coffee. "Married life was a disaster for me. I thought I could make it work with Julieta, but it was unpleasant. She wanted a baby, and I told her that wasn't going to happen. Then my parents joined in. They want grandchildren, and they started asking me for a baby, too."

"What did you do?"

"The whole time I was going to a gay bar. Sometimes I got a little sex in the back room, just a blowjob or a short fuck. The bartender told me that someone was asking questions. Not a policeman, a private investigator. After he said this, I left. I noticed a man in a suit following me. I took the subway to get rid of him. I went all the way to the end of the line, Indios Verdes, and looked around. I didn't see him, but I became paranoid. I thought everyone was following me. I didn't know what to do. I had nowhere to go, because I didn't have any friends."

I gave him a suspicious look and asked, "You have no friends in Mexico City?"

"I grew up with friends, and my whole family lives there, but nobody really knows me the way you do. I went to my parents' house and slept for a long time. I was in bed for days, depressed. I told my mother I had to go back to the United States. She thought I was in love with Moira, poor fool. She and my father had a long argument. He wouldn't look me in the eye. I told Julieta I wanted an *anulación*."

"An annulment?"

"Yes. She agreed to it. My father was very angry. Over and over again, he used the word 'shame' when he talked to my mother. She got emotional, and they would always end up screaming."

"Does your father know anything about you?"

"Only that I didn't want to fuck my wife and I was seen in a gay bar." He went to get some water in the kitchen. He came back and said, "My father wanted to send me to a psychiatrist to 'cure' me. My mother is as innocent as a child, but she knew that was terrible and wouldn't let it happen. One night, she came to my room crying and told me to pack my things. She gave me a bag full of money. She was hiding it in case she had to leave my father in a hurry. She said, 'I'm with that bastard forever now, but you can escape.' I left without saying goodbye to my father. I found out later that he was planning to commit me to a mental hospital the next day."

"That's not legal in California, unless you're a danger to yourself or others. I'm surprised you can do it in Mexico."

"You don't know my father. The word 'legal' means absolutely nothing to him."

"Did you drive straight here?"

"After I crossed the border, I stayed in San Diego for a couple of days. What a nightmare place, a military town, but so very nice." He frowned. "I went through the second border check without a problem. If you look like you have money, they assume you just want to go shopping in LA or something."

"You worked in this country. Don't you have a green card?"

"I do, but if they searched my car, they would have detained me for smuggling currency. It was a lot of money my mother gave me."

"How did you know to come here?"

"I called Moira's phone number, and I heard your voice on the answering machine."

"I'm glad you did. So what do you want to do?"

"I want to get fucked again. And fisted. The rest we can talk about later."

I mixed up some lube and did the best I could, but Temo's hole had indeed gotten tighter while he was away. I tried to put my hand inside him, and it wouldn't fit. After the third attempt I gave up, and Temo broke down. It was the first time I had seen him cry. I held him in my arms and told him it was okay. I told him the reason he couldn't be fisted was that he was under a lot of pressure and felt stressed out. The problem was all in his head. I said, "We can try tomorrow. Let's get some sleep." We hadn't had any dinner, but at that point it was late, and we were both exhausted.

As he dozed off, I heard him say softly, "I love you." I decided that I loved Temo, too. Our sexual attraction was undeniable, and I certainly found him amusing. In a way, he was the man for me. He dominated my emotional life as no one had ever done before, but I still had nagging reservations. A phrase intruded on my thoughts about him and gave me no peace: be careful what you wish for.

I stayed awake for a long time pondering the implications of Temo's last words to me that night. After months of evasion, he finally reached a point where he came out with the truth. He had gotten himself into some kind of trouble and needed my help. In the midst of a melodrama to which I was unaccustomed, I'd have to be patient and wait for him to explain things to me.

∞

I awoke at about seven the next morning to the smell of Temo making coffee. I walked into the kitchen naked and saw him fully dressed. His demeanor had changed completely from the previous night. I tried to embrace him, but he pushed me away and said, "I need to make a phone call. It's private." I went back to bed and fell asleep.

I woke up an hour later to see that Temo had gone. He left a few things around the apartment, including his toothbrush, so I figured he would return soon. I decided to call Raúl.

"Guess who I just saw."

With a sigh he said, "Cuauhtémoc?"

"Yes. He slept in my bed last night." I told Raúl about Temo's arrival, his story of leaving Mexico, and his early morning departure. I said I expected him to return at some point that day, and I was reluctant to leave the apartment, because he had a key.

Raúl said emphatically, "Call a locksmith."

"Why?"

"I always thought that guy had the potential to be a psycho killer. He could be loving one moment, and the next, he looked like he was going to murder me. He's very damaged, and your love is *not* going to fix that."

"I wish you had mentioned this when Moira and I called you last year."

"With him, it's a mystery inside a mystery. Where does it end?"

"Not with bloodshed, I hope."

He asked, "Did you ask him any questions about his past?"

"I didn't have much of an opportunity. When I saw him cry, I didn't want to be too aggressive."

"Temo never cried, not even when I was punching his hole. Something has changed."

I said, "That's what I think. I don't know what to do."

"I'm going to pray for you."

I hung up and went to the door to make sure the deadbolt was locked. I gathered Temo's clothes from around the apartment. I held them to my face and smelled them. I sat down and stared into space for a while, pondering what to do. I decided not to change the locks. I thought if he needed somewhere to stay in an emergency, I didn't mind if he used my place. Then I reconsidered. I said to myself, "Temo has my phone number. He can call before he comes over." As I waited for the locksmith, I took a shower, ate some breakfast, and did the dishes. Changing the deadbolt took about an hour, and it wasn't cheap, but I felt safer when it was done. I called in sick at Libros Revolución and stayed home all day, just in case Temo called. He didn't.

At dusk, I went around the apartment turning on lights, and I saw a note at the base of one of the lamps. I couldn't believe I'd missed it. The note was in the curvy cursive of an adolescent girl. I found it hard to believe it was Temo's handwriting, but it had to have been, because the note was addressed to *Payaso*, the name he used to tease me. The word was crossed out, and the word *AMOR* was written above it. The rest of the note was in English:

> I have to go away for business this morning. I hope I see you again. I want to escape with you, and we can share a perfect life. My dream. I love two people in this world, my mother and you. Remember me. I kiss you, Temo.
>
> P. S. If I don't return, keep everything I left in your apartment.

I shivered when I read this. It sounded like a suicide note to me. I went to bed and slept deeply for a long time.

∞

I came home from work the next day to find that the locks on my door hadn't been disturbed. There was nothing out of place, and there were no messages on my answering machine. I searched the apartment. I found a pair of Temo's socks under my bed and put them with the rest of his clothes in the chest of drawers that Moira had left behind for me to use. In the hall closet, which I rarely opened, I saw a purse, old fashioned, nondescript, and too small to use as a piece of luggage. It must have been the bag his mother had given him. I opened it and found stacks of American money, partly in small denominations, and partly in hundreds. At the very bottom of the bag was a pistol, the kind his mother might have carried for protection, small caliber but capable of doing some damage. I closed the curtains and laid the money out on my bed in stacks. I counted and recounted it: a little over $28,000. I placed the money back in the bag—I didn't touch the pistol—and stashed it with Temo's dirty laundry.

The next week was uneventful, and gradually, I was less and less afraid, until I felt almost nothing except sadness. I thought it was unlikely that I would see Temo again, and even if I did, I suspected it wouldn't be under pleasant circumstances. Every day I checked the phone numbers that appeared on my answering machine in the list of "missed calls." I dialed a few I didn't recognize, only to reach call centers full of people trying to sell life insurance or medicine for erectile dysfunction. I had never taken a picture of Temo, and the mental image I had of him was starting to fade from my mind.

TWENTY

It took me until early July to realize that Bernie wasn't going to leave Los Angeles any time soon. He continued to work at Libros Revolución as though nothing had changed. I asked him about this as tactfully as I could, and he responded indecisively, whining about his finances, and shifting his weight nervously from one foot to the other. He cheered up when I told him, "A lot of my friends moved away recently. I'm happy to have you around."

∞

I received a post card from Moira in Chiapas, and she included the address of the school where she was teaching. I decided to write back and tell her what happened with Temo. I admitted that I missed him and asked if she had a picture she could share. I didn't mention that he had left money and a gun in my apartment, nor did I say I smelled his clothes every so often to bring back memories of him.

A month later, Moira's response arrived: a large envelope containing a letter, a sealed envelope, and a black and white photograph of

Temo. I looked at the last item for some time before I got around to reading the letter. In the picture he wore a dress shirt with a tie, and over it, a vest. He had a very short full beard, but he had taken the time to shave his cheeks to give it a clean line, something he often neglected to do when I knew him. This extra grooming suggested that the photo was taken for a formal event, though he was not wearing a suit. His nose looked a little wider than I remembered, and I regretted not being able to see his profile, which I considered his face's most distinguished and least European trait. He frowned slightly, or perhaps this was merely the effect of the way the facial hair framed his lips. One ear stuck out a bit more than the other, and one eye was slightly lower than the other. I wondered if he was about to raise one eyebrow ever so slightly—a charming habit he had. I found the asymmetry of his face beautiful, but it bothered him in moments of vanity. His prominent eyebrows sat close to his upper eyelids, and made me think he was scowling at the photographer. The eyes, dark brown in real life but black in the photo, had a piercing gaze, one that must have looked hostile to those who didn't know him. Highlights shone on each of his pupils. They were in the shape of windows and gave me the slightest view—the only one I would ever have—of his family home, or so I imagined.

I unfolded Moira's letter and read it:

Dear Guillermito,

I am very happy to hear from you, but sad about the occasion. I assume you haven't heard from Temo yet. If by any chance you do, please contact me immediately. The number of my office is above. You can leave a message that only I will hear. I have no phone at home.

When I got over the shock of hearing about Temo's sex life, I realized that you two were good for each other. You have far more patience for the nonsense that comes out of his mouth, the mood swings, the lack of affection, etc., than I did. What I perceived as your conservatism relative to my politics is really an advantage in dealing with all sorts of people. Like a real Christian, you see good in everyone, a possibility for redemption. But you were raised by atheists. What I am describing—tolerance is too milquetoast a word—allows you to help Temo be a better man.

I was surprised by your suggestion that he might have violent tendencies. Despite his flashes of temper, he seemed like a guy who was never really aggressive. I don't think he was involved in anything illegal, he was just trying to save his life. And he escaped from the clutches of that monster of a father at the last possible moment. I feel for his mother. She must be in agony.

I don't think he ever worked for the CIA, but he was definitely covering something up. Maybe it was the lying you do when you're not comfortable with yourself.

I write all of this in the hope that our Temo is still alive.

Now comes the terrible part. After reading your letter, I did some research. I got help from a colleague who has a sick fascination with Mexican tabloids. He found an article in ¡Alarma! that seems to describe what happened to Temo. This clipping is in the sealed envelope I enclosed. If you decide to open it, please read my thoughts first.

The timeline fits with Temo's disappearance. If he drove to Mexico City and reconciled with his family, he could have been at the scene of the murder reported in the story. The autopsy results, which a reporter bribed a coroner to disclose, are not normally the sort of thing ¡Alarma! troubles itself with, but there was a suspicion that something scandalous could be made of them.

I think the man in the photograph bears a resemblance to Temo, and details in the story correspond with things I heard from him and his parents. Nevertheless, I have my doubts.

The victim is not identified as "Cuauhtémoc" or "Temo" anywhere in the article. He has a completely different name. I don't know what to make of this. Am I obsessing about a coincidence while Temo is alive somewhere in Mexico? Or did he assume another identity when we knew him? Why would he do that? If you think our friend would never use an alias, please don't bother to open the envelope. Throw it into someone else's trash and keep hoping.

One more thought: have you tried email? I know there's no internet at the apartment, and you don't have access through the school anymore, but perhaps you can try at the library. I'm grasping at straws. It hurts me to think that your heart has been broken. Please stay in touch however you can.

Love,

Moira

I put the letter down and thought about whether I'd open the envelope. I decided to test my willpower and take Moira's suggestion about email first. I left the apartment right away. I managed to reach the nearest library a half hour before it closed. I composed a message, striking a tone that was concerned yet not judgmental, and clicked send.

∞

I returned to the library a few days later to see if I had a response. When he lived in Los Angeles, Temo would sometimes answer an email from me within minutes. This time there was nothing, only messages from the Cal Arts Alumni Association asking for a contribution.

∞

Around this time, the first installment of my student loans came due, and I decided to use Temo's money to make the payment. I understood his goodbye note to say that I was welcome to it. I wasn't given to superstition, but in the back of my mind, I harbored a thought that as soon as I took some of the money from his mother's purse, he would return and ask for it back. I laid all of his possessions out on the bed, including the clothes, and looked at them. These things, plus Moira's picture, were the only traces I possessed of a man who rarely left my thoughts since he disappeared. I opened the purse and counted the amount of the loan payment in small denominations. I headed to the post office to get a money order. I experienced a moment of panic when it occurred to me that he might have left me marked bills related to some criminal case. After the clerk at the post office accepted them without a question, I remembered that this was money his mother had set aside little by little, hoarding enough to escape her husband one day. If anything was legal tender, it was this wad of cash. I requested a list of purchase restrictions governing money orders, and I was handed a sheet of paper informing me that anyone buying over $3000 worth of them in one day had to complete a form and show identification.

Back at home, I called the student loan agency to inquire how I could pay off my balance in one lump sum. I was told that student loans, unlike mortgages, reward early repayment. Every penny in excess of the minimum monthly payment would be applied to the principal rather than the interest. I was given an adjusted total I would need to remit in order to discharge the loan, and a date by which the bank would have to receive it.

After that call, I bought just under $3000 in money orders per day at various post offices until I had accumulated enough to make my payment. I placed them in a big envelope with the necessary documents and mailed them a week before the due date. A few days later, I received an acknowledgment that I had paid the balance in full. With that, I felt free from the burden weighing down many art school graduates. To celebrate, I went to the New Beverly Cinema to see *Jackie Brown*. The movie hadn't been a big hit, which surprised me, because I thoroughly enjoyed it, in no small part because I identified with the title character's scheme. Compared to her I was an amateur, but I felt a special appreciation for the delicate manipulations required to start a new life.

∞

I made a last attempt to contact Temo by email, and once again, I got no response. I decided to open the sealed envelope that Moira had sent. There had been periods when I almost succeeded in forgetting that it existed, but something always reminded me, and I would feel a pang of curiosity mixed with guilt. The smell of Temo was almost gone from the clothes I kept in my drawer, and the money (which I had also been using to pay rent) was running low. Soon there would be nothing left of him, aside from a purse and a gun, neither of which I intended to use, and a photograph that appeared a little more worn every time I looked at it.

I tore open the envelope to find a lurid front page from *¡Alarma!* with a headline reading *Visita Fatal a Iztapalapa*. The story recounted a brutal murder in a poor suburb of Mexico City. In the photo, a man lay face down on the sidewalk in a large pool of blood. According to the article, he had been shot at point blank range by an unknown assailant around eleven o'clock at night. I scrutinized the image of the victim. Everything in the man's face sagged, and whatever had animated it—how he smiled when he saw a loved one or laughed when he heard a good joke—had drained away, leaving dead weight. When I looked at this face, I choked up and felt a wave of pity, regardless of who this person was. I couldn't see Temo in the photo. Perhaps it had been too long and my memory of him was no longer reliable. The only part of the picture I recognized immediately was a necklace with an image of the Virgin of Guadalupe, the one Temo always wore. But surely there were many men in Mexico who owned exactly the same necklace, I thought to myself. I searched the article for telling details. The name of the victim wasn't the name of the man I knew, just as Moira had told me. The information about his family was generic. The only extraordinary thing was the mention of an *ano infundibular* noted at the autopsy. From the context, I understood that this identified the victim as an "anal compulsive homosexual." The writer concluded that the young man in the picture had been cruising, and rather than a fuck, he got a bullet in the back. Could this have been Temo? I couldn't say beyond doubt that it wasn't, but I remained unconvinced. I called Moira's answering machine in Chiapas and told her what I thought about the article she sent me. I had to resign myself to uncertainty about what had happened to the man I loved.

∞

In September, the worst of the summer heat arrived. For days on end, sleeping was difficult at night, and by nine in the morning the sun was blazing hot. One evening I returned to my stifling apartment to hear Gregorio leaving a message on my answering machine. I picked up the phone before he hung up. "Hey, how are you? It must be awful in Santa Clarita."

He said, "Hot as hell, but it's great for oil painting. The canvases dry so fast."

I asked, "Do you want to get together before school starts?"

"That's why I called." We made a date for the next evening.

When Gregorio arrived at my door, I could hardly believe my eyes. He had cut off all his wild hair, and there was no makeup on his face. We hugged and kissed, and I said, "I like your new look."

"Thanks. I decided to make a change for my last semester."

I suggested we have dinner at our regular spot, and we walked down the hill. I waited until we ordered to ask him, "Are you going to Berlin after you graduate?"

"Yeah, I'm planning to move after I see my family at Christmas. They totally disapprove, but that makes me want to do it more. I miss Winston so much."

"I'm proud of you. I think it's the right choice. How is Winston?"

Gregorio smiled. "He's fine, enjoying his life as a rising art star."

"I'm sorry I've been out of touch with you two lately." I told him the whole story of Temo.

"Man, that's terrible. Sounds like a *telenovela*."

"I know you never liked him, but I did… a lot." We were silent for a moment as our food arrived and we began eating. "He left me so suddenly. I think he must still be alive somewhere. Moira thinks he was murdered in Mexico City." I shrugged and looked down at the table. "She may be right."

"Poor guy. I didn't know."

"Be good to Winston. Or I guess I should say Andë."

"He's still Winston to me. Everyone else can call him by that other name."

"Are you ready for Berlin? It'll be cold there when you arrive, as hard as that is to imagine right now. The days will be short."

"Ugh, don't remind me. I need to buy more warm clothes." He paused and said, "You should come visit us."

"I'd like that. One day."

"Maybe it's too soon to tell you this, but I think you should write something about Temo. You were always good at that."

"Do you mean I'm not really an artist?"

"That's not what I'm saying." He looked me in the eye and said seriously, "Maybe it's the best way to get over everything you've been through."

"Well, I'll think about it." I didn't say that I'd already started putting my thoughts on paper.

After dinner, as we were saying our goodbyes, Gregorio gave me a present. He said, "You can open it after I've left."

"Thanks." Tears came to my eyes, and I said, "I should go. Take care." We kissed and hugged, and in a minute, he was gone.

I opened the package as soon as I got inside. It was a gouache by Gregorio of our whole group of friends in my apartment, based on the photo he took of us smiling for the camera at Christmastime. He had added Frances and Carmen to the scene. The painting was in a nice frame, probably a thrift store purchase. On the back was a handwritten note: "Happy times, full of love."

I Should Have Known Better was funded through an Indiegogo campaign that ran for the duration of February 2021.

William E. Jones and We Heard You Like Books offer many thanks to the following individuals:

Dave Asselin, Craig Carroll, Ashley Gorton, Brian Wescott, bjc, Ernesto D Ayala, kinofalke, Evan Purchell, Matthew Carson, Tausif Noor, Adam Possehl, Wes Del Val, Chadwick Roberts, emre busse, Rita Raley, youthtobaccomovement, Macartney Morris, Jose Guerrero, abilows, S Schtinter, Nick Toti, Kaj-anne Pepper, Christopher Yin, emil lazar, Carson Parish, Sohum Pal, Xavier Espejo, Andrew O Byrne, Farhad Mirza, Shiv Kotecha, Evan Neuhausen, Damir Avdagic, Nikki Woods, hedi el kholti, Raymond Villescas, ereckjarvis, ave.barr, jauman, Deric Carner, Vincent Passerat, Murray Anderson, mroeder74, William G Thelen, Jory Mickelson, Greg Goldberg, jesse.ataide, Thomas Scutt, Robbie Trocchia, sam, Dicky Bahto, Jason Alba, Timothy Nassau, John Matkowsky, Peter Stauffer, Doug Boney, Alex Lake, Isabelle E Hogenkamp, Davide Savorani, Anthony Raynal, pcmeshaw, khenderson11, Anand Pandya, Matthew Lawrence, Court Cline, Martin Marafioti, Scott Cameron Weaver, motnedwob, Daniel Humphrey, juditheisler, Thomas Moore, erika.balsom, migiwaorimo, Ian Dempsey, Michael Goebel, Henrik Mjönes, Minus Plato, David Joselit,

Tiger Munson, Jeffrey Ostergren, Anne Collier, Paul Moreno, Timothy Peyton, Matthew Brannon, Julian Pozzi, Margie Schnibbe, Chris Behroozian, Juan Barquin, Karen Lofgren, Stephen Hepworth, Violet Hopkins, Seth Tisue, Tomas Trussow, Nathan Rouse, Stephen Biga, Adam Baran, Robert Moore, Charchi Stinson, JC Pavon, Bradford Nordeen, Michael Fahy, Ford Thomas, Kel R Karpinski, Caden Gardner, Peter Sotos, Aaron Lecklider, David Inniss, Matthew Limpede, Justin Lincoln, Tricia Paik, Mike Lamb, Photios Giovanis, Stuart Comer, Sarah Workneh, Dave Ehrlich, Blue S. Biga, Aubrey Longley-Cook, Yossi Milo, Laurie Nye, Raffaella Cortese, Brittany Miller, Em Cru, Jason Hanasik, Louis Valenzuela, Thomas Hull, zoecwalsh, Amanda Ross-Ho, oliviamole, joe, adschur, dettenogle, inezparra, rrprr, malaiqbal, DAVID KORDANSKY GALLERY, INC., Eric Dinsmore, Joshua Isaac, Alex Clausen, Steven Bachrach, daniel sander, Adam Boon, Morgan Thomas, Mark Harvey, Douglas Morales, Henri Savikko, Eric Murga, Ivy Pochoda, Augie Robles, Karl McCool, Rebecca Koblick, Dorthe Nors, Angela Dufresne, J T, Commonwealth and Council, Nate Lippens, Barbara Cottle, Enrique Castrejon, Gabriel E. Flores, Jameson Fitzpatrick, Christopher O'Halloran, sami.brussels, Panos Giannikopoulos, Stephen Trull, and Robert Berens.